Finding
Courage
by

Kathi Daley

I want to thank the very talented Jessica Fischer for the cover art.

I so appreciate Bruce Curran, who is always ready and willing to answer my cyber questions; Jayme Maness for helping out with the book clubs; and Peggy Hyndman for helping sleuth out those pesky typos.

And, of course, thanks to the readers and bloggers in my life, who make doing what I do possible.

Thank you to Randy Ladenheim-Gil for the editing.

And finally, I want to thank my husband Ken for allowing me time to write by taking care of everything else.

Books by Kathi Daley

Come for the murder, stay for the romance.

Zoe Donovan Cozy Mystery:

Halloween Hijinks
The Trouble With Turkeys
Christmas Crazy
Cupid's Curse
Big Bunny Bump-off
Beach Blanket Barbie
Maui Madness
Derby Divas
Haunted Hamlet
Turkeys, Tuxes, and Tabbies
Christmas Cozy
Alaskan Alliance
Matrimony Meltdown
Soul Surrender
Heavenly Honeymoon
Hopscotch Homicide
Ghostly Graveyard
Santa Sleuth
Shamrock Shenanigans
Kitten Kaboodle
Costume Catastrophe
Candy Cane Caper
Holiday Hangover
Easter Escapade
Camp Carter
Trick or Treason
Reindeer Roundup
Hippity Hoppity Homicide

Firework Fiasco
Henderson House

Zimmerman Academy The New Normal
Ashton Falls Cozy Cookbook

Tj Jensen Paradise Lake Mysteries by Henery Press:

Pumpkins in Paradise
Snowmen in Paradise
Bikinis in Paradise
Christmas in Paradise
Puppies in Paradise
Halloween in Paradise
Treasure in Paradise
Fireworks in Paradise
Beaches in Paradise

Whales and Tails Cozy Mystery:

Romeow and Juliet
The Mad Catter
Grimm's Furry Tail
Much Ado About Felines
Legend of Tabby Hollow
Cat of Christmas Past
A Tale of Two Tabbies
The Great Catsby
Count Catula
The Cat of Christmas Present
A Winter's Tail
The Taming of the Tabby
Frankencat

The Cat of Christmas Future
Farewell to Felines
A Whisker in Time – *September 2018*
The Catsgiving Feast – *November 2018*

Writers' Retreat Southern Seashore Mystery:
First Case
Second Look
Third Strike
Fourth Victim
Fifth Night
Sixth Cabin
Seventh Chapter

Rescue Alaska Paranormal Mystery:
Finding Justice
Finding Answers
Finding Courage
Finding Christmas – *November 2018*

A Tess and Tilly Mystery:
The Christmas Letter
The Valentine Mystery
The Mother's Day Mishap
The Halloween House
The Thanksgiving Trip – *October 2018*

Haunting by the Sea:
Homecoming by the Sea

Secrets by the Sea
Missing by the Sea – *October 2018*
Christmas by the Sea – *December 2018*

Sand and Sea Hawaiian Mystery:
Murder at Dolphin Bay
Murder at Sunrise Beach
Murder at the Witching Hour
Murder at Christmas
Murder at Turtle Cove
Murder at Water's Edge
Murder at Midnight

Seacliff High Mystery:
The Secret
The Curse
The Relic
The Conspiracy
The Grudge
The Shadow
The Haunting

Road to Christmas Romance:
Road to Christmas Past

Chapter 1

Saturday, October 13

His pulse quickened as they approached. He'd waited so long. Too long. He closed his eyes and reveled in the memory, which didn't come as a gentle wave but as a surge of agony from the depths of his personal hell. He'd craved the searing pain, the deeply felt anguish. It was only during these moments, when he was sure he would drown in a river of longing, that he felt truly alive.

On the surface, the rescue seemed fairly routine. Two teenage boys had gone hiking earlier that morning. They were only supposed to be gone a couple of hours but had failed to return by the time they'd agreed to meet with the families for lunch. The father of one of the boys had gone looking for them, and when he was unable to find them after a couple of hours, he'd called the Rescue Alaska Search and Rescue Team, of which I, Harmony Carson, am a member. It was fall in Alaska, which meant the days were becoming shorter toward the endless night of winter. Although the daytime temperatures were mild for this time of the year, the overnight low promised to dip well below freezing. Normally, we like to interview the person making the call, but the man said he was heading toward Devil's Gulch, where he was certain the boys had been planning to hike, and the reception there was sketchy, so the information we had to go on was limited. By the time the call came through, the sun had begun its descent toward the jagged peak of the distant mountain, so we knew there was no time to lose.

Jake Cartwright, my close friend and brother-in-law, had taken the call. I was already at Neverland, the bar Jake owned and where I worked as a waitress, as was S&R team member Wyatt Forrester, who worked part time there as a bartender. Jake had made a quick decision to employ the team members present to look for the boys, so he and his S&R dog, Sitka, me and my S&R dog, Yukon, Wyatt, and team member Austin Brown, who happened to be in the bar having a drink, set off with a feeling of urgency, given the sharp drop in temperature and impending darkness.

"Jake to Harmony," Jake said over the two-way radio we all carried as we traveled toward our destination.

"Go for Harmony," I answered. We'd spread out to cover more ground in the event the boys had either doubled back or taken another route. We knew if we didn't find them before then, once we reached the narrow entrance to the gulch, we'd all converge into a single unit.

"Have you managed to pick up anything?" Jake referred to my ability to psychically connect to those victims I was meant to help rescue. My ability, which I oftentimes considered a curse, had come to me during the lowest point in my life. My sister Val, who had become my guardian after our parents were killed in an accident, had gone out on a rescue. She'd become lost in a storm, and although the team tried to find her, they came up with nothing but dead ends. She was the first person I connected to, and the one I most wanted to save. I couldn't save Val, but since then, I've used my gift to locate and rescue dozens of people. I couldn't save them all, but today, I was determined that our search would lead us to the missing boys.

"No," I answered, frustration evident in my voice. "Which is odd. Even if the boys are uninjured, they must be scared. The temperature has dropped and the sun is beginning to set. The fact that I'm not getting anything at all is concerning me."

There are really only three reasons I can think of when I don't pick up something, even a small whisper, during a rescue. The most common is that the person who's been reported missing isn't really missing at all. They might not have checked in with the person who reported them missing, but they were perfectly safe, not in physical pain or mental duress. I hoped that would turn out to be the case with these two boys.

The second commonest reason I'm unable to pick up a psychic connection is because the person I'm trying to reach is either unconscious or already dead. That's the reason I least hope to confirm, but at times, the person we're trying to find has already taken his final breath before we even begin our search.

And the third reason I'm occasionally unable to make a connection is because the person in need of rescue senses me but is blocking me. This rarely occurs, but it's possible.

"Is Sitka picking up anything?" I asked. Even if I was unable to connect, I'd think Sitka would pick up something. We didn't have anything with the boys' scent to help direct the dogs today, so they'd been instructed to find anyone who might be in the area. Having a specific scent to track worked a lot better, but at this time of the year, when there weren't many people out hiking, if anyone was around, the dogs should be able to locate them.

"No. Nothing specific at least, but he does seem to sense someone," Jake answered. "If the boys came this way, as the father seemed to think they had, he'll find them. If they veered off in another direction, though, we might have a real problem. Given the anticipated overnight temps, it's important to find them as quickly as possible. We're going to go on, but I'd like you to take a short break and really try to connect. If you sense something, let us know."

"Okay." I stopped walking and looked around. "I don't have a lot to go on, but I'll try."

"The man I spoke to said the boys' names are Mark and Andrew. They're both fourteen and have dark hair and dark eyes. That's all I got from him before he cut out."

I signed off, then sat down on a large rock. I instructed Yukon to sit and stay next to me, then I closed my eyes. I relaxed my mind and focused on the information I had. Mark and Andrew. Scared, most likely. Possibly injured. Dark hair, dark eyes.

Nothing. Absolutely nothing.

I tried again. I allowed whatever images that came to me to pass through my mind. I hoped if they were out there, their psyches would somehow find mine.

Still nothing.

I had an intuition that the man who'd called Jake to report the missing teens had been less than honest. If I had to guess, this whole thing was a hoax. It happened from time to time, although I had no idea why anyone would do such a thing. Still, if the boys actually were in the area and were in some sort of trouble, it was likely I'd pick up an echo of fear if nothing else. I was about to give up my quest to make a connection and had stood up to move on when a feeling of sorrow pierced my heart with such intensity it left me gasping for air.

Oh God. My hand clenched my chest.

My instinct was to break the connection, but I knew if I wanted to locate the source of the pain I needed to maintain it, so I took a deep breath and opened my heart to the anguish. I allowed the pain to envelop me as I tried to figure out who it was I'd connected to. I could sense the distress was emotional rather than physical. Someone was dealing with intense grief. No, not grief, longing. The suffering was deep and real, but there was something else as well. I frowned. In the midst of the sorrow was anticipation.

I focused harder. I knew I hadn't connected to the boys but someone else. Someone older. I could sense a darkness. An emptiness. As if the soul of the person

I'd connected with had been drained of all life. I felt the individual try to pull back. He knew I'd made a connection and was trying to push me away, but I resisted. I tried to go deeper, but then I saw it. My eyes flew open.

My hand flew to my mouth. I was sure I was going to be sick, but I thrust the nausea aside. "Harmony to Jake."

"Go for Jake."

"It's a trap. Pull back. Pull back now."

In that instant, there was a loud crash as the mountain above the narrow opening to the gulch exploded, sending tons of dirt and rock to the path below. I turned and ran as fast as I could. Tears streamed down my face, but I didn't really notice. I felt fear, and pain, and death.

Oh God.

I ran faster still. Yukon was running in front of me. He must have sensed where to go because he never wavered. When I arrived at the place where the dirt and rock had settled, I found Sitka standing over Jake, who appeared to be unconscious.

"Jake." I ran to where he was lying on the hard ground and felt for a pulse. I let out a breath of relief when I saw he had one. He had a bump on his head but appeared to be otherwise uninjured. I grabbed my radio and called Sarge, who was holding down the fort at the base. "Harmony to Sarge."

"Go for Sarge."

"There's been an accident. A landslide. Find Jordan. Have her meet Dani at the helipad. We're going to need an air evacuation. And Sarge, tell them to hurry."

With that, I stood up and slowly looked around. I wasn't sure where Austin and Wyatt were. Had they been with Jake? In front of him? On another trail altogether?

I heard Jake groan. I turned to find both Sitka and Yukon licking his face. I knelt down next to him. "Are you okay?"

Jake put his hand to his head. "What happened?"

"Landslide. You were hit in the head with something. You blacked out but appear to be otherwise okay. Where were Wyatt and Austin before the mountain came down?"

Jake sat up. His face paled. "In front of me."

I looked down at Sitka and Yukon. "Find Wyatt. Find Austin."

The dogs ran on ahead, and I knew I needed to follow, but the dizziness and nausea I'd kept at bay had returned. I was fine, I reminded myself. I'd seen something I'd need to process, but the most important thing was to find my friends. I stood up and looked at the spot in front of me, where the trail had once been. This was bad. Really bad.

It didn't take the dogs long to find Wyatt. He'd managed to find a place next to the wall of the canyon to crouch down, avoiding most of the debris from above. After a bit of back and forth, we determined he was trapped and hurt. Jake managed to get up despite his head injury to help me dig him out. It was a long, arduous process because each rock needed to be lifted and set aside. I don't know how we found the strength to do it, but when I saw Wyatt's face, bruised but alert, I wanted to cry in relief.

His leg was broken and his shoulder dislocated but he didn't appear to have any life-threatening injuries. By the time Jake and I had freed him, the sun had set, but we could hear Dani's chopper in the distance. I wasn't sure I had any strength left, but we weren't done. "Find Austin," I said to the dogs, even though I suspected he was gone. I'd been able to sense Wyatt as the dogs looked for him, but when I focused on Austin, all I found was silence. Of course, if he was unconscious I might not be able to make a connection, so there was that hope for me to cling to. I tried to keep up as the dogs scrambled over the rubble. Wyatt hadn't been all that far in front of Jake and so hadn't been in the area of largest destruction, but the farther toward the center of the landslide the dogs traveled, the more certain I was Austin was gone. By the time Dani had landed the chopper, Sitka alerted. He'd found Austin.

Sometimes all you can do is what you have to do. Dani had brought Jordan and Sarge with her, so they helped load Wyatt into the chopper, where Jordan went to work on his injuries. Once Wyatt was in Jordan's hands, Dani and Sarge helped us retrieve Austin's body. When we'd freed him from the rubble, it was completely dark and the temperature had dropped at least thirty degrees. Jake was still dizzy from his head injury, and we couldn't all fit in the chopper at the same time, so Jordan went with Dani, who flew Wyatt and Jake to the hospital, while Sarge waited with the dogs and me. Austin's body would be airlifted down as well, but it was more important to see to the injured.

"It wasn't an accident," I said to Sarge after we'd built a fire for warmth, then settled in to wait for Dani to come back for us.

"What do you mean, it wasn't an accident?"

I tilted up my head so I could more clearly see the northern lights overhead. I wanted to embrace the breathtaking beauty that could be found in the Alaskan wilderness, but all I could feel was grief. "In the brief moment before the mountain exploded, I connected with someone in so much pain it was almost unbearable. I felt the rawness of exposed emotion as grief was channeled into rage." I lowered my head and looked at Sarge. "Someone lured us up here. Someone set off explosives and intentionally caused the landslide. I have no doubt the intention was to bury us all, but I'd stopped to try to make a connection, so I was well behind the others. When I realized what was happening, I was able to warn Jake, which gave him maybe a second to retreat." I swallowed as a lump of emotion clogged my throat. "Jake told me that he'd called to the others, but the mountain was already coming down and they were too far ahead."

Sarge was silent for a moment. I imagined he needed that time to try to process what I'd just said. To lose a member of the team to a random landslide was bad enough; to lose him to a madman was another thing entirely. "So you're saying Austin was murdered."

I nodded. "Yes. That's what I'm saying." I took a deep breath as my entire body began to shake.

"Are you okay?" Sarge looked me in the eye. He put his hands on my shoulders and gave me a little shake.

"I'm okay. It's just that…" I couldn't continue. I tried to speak, but at that moment I couldn't even breathe. I felt my heart pounding in my chest as a flash of memory seared through my mind.

"Just that what?" Sarge said persuasively. "You didn't finish what you were saying."

I shook my head. I couldn't speak. I didn't want to remember.

"You know you can trust me."

I nodded. Sitka and Yukon were sitting so close to me, they were practically in my lap. I could sense their distress. I needed to pull myself together, but I wasn't sure how I was going to do that.

"I want to help you, but you need to finish your thought," Sarge insisted.

I put my arms around the dogs and took comfort in their warmth. I let them lick the tears from my face, and then I answered. Softly at first, but as my voice found its footing, I went on with more intensity. "In that moment, when I connected to whoever set off the dynamite that caused the landslide, I saw something else. A memory. Not my memory, *his* memory."

Sarge frowned. "Okay. What was it?"

"It was Val." I felt my body begin to shake again. "He was with her. The man who killed Austin was with Val when she died."

Chapter 2

Sunday, October 14

I'd called my best friend, Chloe Rivers, while Sarge and I were waiting for Dani to return. I briefly explained the landslide, and she not only offered words of comfort but volunteered to go over to my place to let the dogs out and feed all the animals. I was grateful for her help; by the time I'd finally made it home to the cabin I share with seven dogs, four cats, eight rabbits, and a blind mule named Homer, it was well past midnight.

Wyatt had been checked into the hospital in Fairbanks. Jordan had wanted Jake to spend a night there as well, but he'd finally convinced her that he'd be fine at home with his own personal doctor and girlfriend to watch over him. After Austin's body had been taken to the local funeral home, Jake had met briefly with Officer Hank Houston. The plan they'd come up with was for all of us to meet with Houston the following morning, after we'd had a chance to rest and deal with our grief over the loss of a team member and friend.

Sarge and I had talked about it and decided not to tell Jake about my vision relating to Val until the following day, which I guess at that point was today. We figured he already had a lot to deal with, and we knew he was going to take the possibility that Val might have been murdered harder than anyone else. Of course, I still wasn't sure exactly what the vision meant. The flash had been brief but very real.

Over the course of the past thirteen years, I'd relived Val's final breaths in my thoughts and dreams a million times. I remembered being scared and wanting to be with her, to offer whatever comfort I could. I remembered wanting to have the chance to tell her I loved her, to ensure that she knew how much she'd meant to me. And then she was there, in my mind. I knew she'd felt me as I'd felt her. I'd been with her as she died. The memory was permanently etched in my mind, so I knew what I was seeing when the image of the exact same scene had flashed through my mind last night. Only this time I hadn't been viewing it through my eyes but through *his*.

We all believed Val had been lost in the storm. But had she? Maybe the man who'd caused Austin's death had kidnapped her. Maybe he'd taken her up the mountain to the cave where her body had been found and killed her. Or maybe she'd been lost in the storm and taken refuge in the cave. Maybe the man was lost as well and just happened to stumble onto the same cave she had. Unlikely, I admitted, but possible. The only way we could know for certain was to capture the man and make him tell us. That was something I was either going to do or die trying.

I needed to sleep, but it wouldn't come. Every time I closed my eyes, I saw the mountain coming down, Austin's lifeless eyes, and Val's last breath as she passed into the next life. To say that the evening had been an emotional one was an understatement. At this point I merely felt numb, but I knew once the numbness wore off, I was going to have more to deal with than I expected to be able to handle.

Moose, my therapy cat, had spent a good part of the night curled up on the sofa with me. That was unusual for the cantankerous old feline who seemed to have come into my life to keep my emotions balanced. While he seemed to be willing to do his job when needed, he wasn't the sort to cuddle or linger once it was done.

The dogs, sensing my distress, had also stayed nearby, so it was a crowded sofa where I huddled and waited out the night. As first light rolled around, I was more than ready to get out of my tiny cabin for a long walk in the woods. The sky was dark with heavy clouds and the temperature lingered just below freezing, so I bundled up, then grabbed my rifle and set out with the seven dogs.

Yukon, the shelter dog I was training for search and rescue, normally settled into a position in the front of the pack, with my wolf hybrid, Denali, and my husky mix, Shia. My two retired sled dogs, Juno and Kodi, usually were in the middle of the pack, while three-legged Lucky and golden retriever Honey stayed within an arm's length of me. We'd had a few light snows during the month, although the heavier ones of winter had yet to make their first appearances.

Areas that saw a lot of sun, such as the meadow behind my home, were free of snow, but there was some on the ground in the shade under the trees. It was in one of those shady areas that I first saw footprints. Large footprints. From a boot. At least a size twelve, I decided. The dogs didn't seem to be on alert, as they would be had someone still been around, but given the day before, I cradled my rifle, called the dogs to my side, and headed back to the cabin to call Houston to come and take a look.

******

"When was the last time you were out here before this morning?" Houston asked.

"Yesterday morning."

"And the footprints weren't here?"

I shook my head. "No. Living out in the middle of nowhere this way, I keep an eye out for any signs that I may have had a visitor. I would have noticed the footprints if they'd been here yesterday. These had to have been left sometime between around eight o'clock yesterday morning and this morning, right before I called you."

Houston bent down and took a closer look. "I'm going to take some photos and a cast. When I'm done, I'll come by your cabin and we can talk about what these footprints might mean."

"I need to feed the animals and then clean cat boxes and the barn. I'm going to grab a shower after that. If I'm in the shower when you show up, just come on in. The dogs know you. I think it'll be fine."

Houston looked directly at Denali, who considered it his personal mission to keep me safe. "Are you sure?"

"I'm sure." I touched Houston's arm, then looked directly at Denali. "Friend. Houston is a friend."

Denali wagged his tail, then came forward for a body rub, which, he'd learned along the way, he could expect from anyone who was introduced as a friend.

When I finished with the feeding and cleaning, Houston was just finishing up as well. I told him to help himself to some coffee while I took a quick shower and got dressed. What I didn't expect was that he'd make breakfast while I was getting ready to tackle the day ahead.

"You cooked." I took an appreciative sniff of the wonderful scent coming from the oven.

"I tossed together a breakfast casserole from ingredients I found on hand. I hope you don't mind."

"Mind? I'm grateful." I furrowed a brow. "I guess I never did get around to eating dinner yesterday. No wonder I'm so hungry."

"We're meeting with Jake and the others in a couple of hours, but as long as I'm here and have garnered your attention with my fabulous cooking skills, I wanted to talk to you first." Houston glanced toward the door. "Kojak is in the truck. Is it okay if I bring him in?"

"Of course. I had no idea he was out there or I would have suggested you bring him in earlier."

"He's used to waiting in the car for me when I have to go out on a call, but he knows you and your dogs, so I'm sure he'd appreciate coming in to say hi. I'll get him, and we can talk while we eat."

Houston returned with the rescue I'd hooked him up with and the casserole was done, so we filled our plates and sat down at the small dining table near the window.

"This is really good," I said after taking my first bite. "I want the recipe."

"No recipe. I just use whatever's on hand and mix it all together. I call it breakfast surprise and it's different every time."

"Well, this particular combination is wonderful. So, what did you want to know?"

Houston set down his fork and took a sip of his coffee. "Let's talk about the boot prints. Any idea who they might belong to?"

I took another bite of my food, then leaned back in my chair as I considered the question. "I don't have any neighbors who are close enough to wander around on my property on any sort of a regular basis. If you keep going along the path where I found the prints, it comes out at a fairly large natural pond. I suppose it's possible someone parked on the road, then cut through my property to get to the pond when I wasn't home yesterday. It sort of looked like the footprints came from the woods and then stopped on the edge of my meadow, however."

"It does appear as if whoever left the prints came toward the house from the woods. The snow ends with the tree line, so the person could have continued on farther onto your property."

"The dogs would have gone crazy if that happened, though I wasn't home yesterday afternoon or evening, so there's no way for me to know if they did. I know no one got into the house or the barn; there would have been bloodshed by whichever dog happened to get his teeth into the prowler. Still, I suppose they could have had a look around outside. The question is who and why?"

"What time did you leave home yesterday?"

"Around one. Neverland opens at two on Saturdays. I would have gotten off at ten, but we had the rescue, or I guess I should say the fake rescue. I didn't get home until after one. I usually take a break halfway through my shift to come here to let the dogs out, but when I knew I wouldn't make it, I called Chloe, who came by to let them out at around eight. She didn't mention anything strange going on. If the dogs had sensed an intruder earlier in the day, Denali at the very least would have been extra cautious when Chloe came by. She didn't mention anything about it, but I can ask her."

"We will. But let's finish this conversation first."

"Okay," I agreed. "What else do you want to know?"

Houston got up to refill his coffee, motioning to me. I nodded, and he refilled my cup as well. "When I spoke to Jake last night," he said as he sat down again, "he told me you'd made a connection with someone on the mountain seconds before it exploded and rained down on them."

"Yes, that's correct. I was trying to connect with the boys we'd been sent to find but wasn't getting anything. Time was of the essence with the temperature drop forecasted, so I was trying extra hard to open my mind to any source of pain or fear. In the moment before the rocks and dirt came down on Wyatt and Austin, I connected with someone in a great degree of emotional distress. The emotions that person was experiencing were raw and very intense.

For a second, it felt as if someone had stabbed a knife into my chest, before he seemed to channel all that pain and grief into a single action. It was then I realized what he planned to do. I called Jake and told him to run. He tried to warn the others, but they were too far ahead of him."

"So killing them served as some sort of an emotional release?"

I paused before answering. "I guess you could say that. When he went for the dynamite, I lost the connection, so I can't say for certain how he felt after he sent the mountain rumbling down to the path below, but I think you're right. I think he let his pain build to a point and then channeled it into rage, which he used to kill a target."

"Did you pick up anything at all that might help us to identify him? He seemed to have targeted your group. It stands to reason he must know one or more of you on some level. Maybe he was the subject of a past rescue?"

"I don't know who it was. I picked up emotion, even a memory, but not a face or any physical features. I guess I don't even know for certain it was a man and not a woman, but my sense is that it was a man."

Houston crossed his arms on the table and leaned forward just a bit. "You said you picked up a memory. Your memory or his?"

"Both." I explained my memory of Val's last breaths and how he'd had the same one just before he blew the mountain.

Houston placed his hand on mine. "Oh, Harm, I'm so very sorry. That must have been very painful for you."

I swiped at a tear that threatened to trail down my cheek. "It wasn't fun, but I'll deal with it. What I really want to know is what it means. Did he stumble upon Val and he was trying to help her when she died? Did he kill her? Was she ever lost in the storm at all, or did he kidnap her and then take her to the cave where she was found? This opens up a lot of questions as to what happened that night. It also makes me wonder if what happened last night is somehow linked to Val's death."

Houston frowned. "Jake didn't mention the connection with Val when I spoke to him last night."

"That's because I haven't told him about the memory yet. He loved Val very much. He's going to take this hard. I figured he had enough to deal with last night. I'm going to tell him when I see him today."

Houston got up from the table and started to clear it, and I got up to help. "Is there anything at all you want to tell me before we meet with the group?" he asked.

"I don't know. I don't think so. My mind is humming at a pace that doesn't really allow me to process anything. Austin is dead." I looked Houston in the eye. "Dead. I'll never hear another of his goofy jokes or see his cockeyed grin. How could this happen? Why did it happen? It makes no sense."

Houston put his arms around me and gave me a long hug. He didn't say anything, but I knew he was hurting for me. For all of us. There was nothing I could do to bring Austin back, but I sure as heck could do something about finding his killer. Anger was my friend. When I was angry, I could deal with my grief. I thought back to the man who'd caused the landslide and realized that, as disturbing as it might seem, he'd also found a way to channel his grief into anger. I wondered what had set this chain of events into motion in the first place. Had he suffered a loss he was unable to deal with? Had his anger turned to rage and eventually into vengeance? And what did that have to do with Val?

Chapter 3

It was a somber group who gathered at Neverland later that morning. Jake had put out a sign, letting people know the bar would be closed for a few days. I think he rightfully felt we all needed time to begin to heal before attempting to resume our lives. Wyatt was still in the hospital, but Landon, who had been in Anchorage and had missed yesterday's rescue altogether, had flown back, so there were seven of us sitting around a table.

Jake started things off. "You all know how important this debrief and strategy session is." He looked at Jordan, then Dani, then Sarge, then me. "For those of us who lived through it, talking about it is going to be difficult." Jake looked at Landon, then Houston. "For those of you who didn't, it's going to be even more difficult as you struggle to understand how this tragedy could have occurred. I'm going to turn this over to Officer Houston, but as always, if you have something to say, say it. Holding back never accomplishes anything worthwhile."

I glanced at Sarge. Should I jump right in or wait? He nodded, so I took a breath and jumped in. "I have something," I said. I looked at Jake. "I'm wondering if we should speak in private."

Jake frowned. "Private? Why?"

"When I connected to whoever set off the dynamite that sent the mountain down, I saw something. Something I didn't mention last night."

Jake hesitated. "Okay. Does that pertain to anyone in this room?"

I shook my head. "Not in this room. But it's something that will affect you more than the others."

"Just tell us what you know, Harm. We're a family here. We don't keep secrets."

I took a breath, then swallowed. "When I connected briefly with the man on the mountain, I not only shared his pain and rage, I shared a memory. His memory."

Jake smiled. "That's good. It could help us figure out who he is."

"Maybe. But his memory was also my memory." I glanced at Sarge one more time. He nodded again, so I continued. "Jake, the man was with Val when she died."

The entire room was silent. Everyone looked at Jake, who'd gone pale.

"He was with Val?" Jake croaked.

"In the last second before he blew up the mountain, a flash of memory crossed his mind. It was a memory of Val taking her last breaths. It was the same memory I've had of her all these years. I

30

experienced Val's death in my mind, but he was there. I'm sure of it."

"Maybe your own memory got tangled up with everything else. It was a pretty intense few minutes."

I shook my head. "No. I was in his head. I saw it through his eyes. He was there."

Again, no one spoke. I don't think anyone knew what to say. I sensed Houston was thinking about jumping in, but I shook my head slightly, to let him know he should wait. He was new to the group, and my vision deeply affected everyone at the table who'd known Val, which didn't include him.

Eventually, Dani spoke. "Are you saying the man who sent the mountain down killed Val?"

"I don't know. I only saw a flash. I don't know if he killed her or just happened to be with her. I've been asking myself whether he kidnapped her and took her to the cave where we found her body, or if she really did get lost and he stumbled across her. I can't know unless I can figure out a way to get into his head again."

"We need to find this guy," Landon said.

Jake still sat silently, devoid of color but seemingly intent on what we were saying. I imagined he was questioning everything he thought he knew, just as I had.

"I'm new here and don't want to step on anyone's toes," Houston started off, "but I think we can all agree that finding this man and bringing him to justice is our priority. To do that, we need a place to start looking."

"We need a suspect list," I said.

"This man is most likely known to one or all of you," Houston said. "If Harmony did experience a memory yesterday, it sounds as if he was around when Val died thirteen years ago. That's not a great starting point, but it's something. We'll make a list of every possible person you can think of, then I'll start getting alibis and eliminating them."

It was slow going, getting those first couple of names on a whiteboard, but once we got started, there were over twenty names on the list within the first thirty minutes.

"Do any of these men wear a size twelve boot?" Houston asked.

Dani raised a brow. "A size twelve boot? The guy was up on the mountain. None of us saw him. How can you know what size boot he wore?"

Houston looked at me.

"I had a prowler," I admitted. "I don't know when exactly, and I don't think they got close to the house, but when I walked the dogs this morning, I noticed boot prints in the snow where it hadn't melted."

"Do you think it was the guy?" Jordan asked.

"Probably not. It was probably a fisherman or a hiker. I called Houston just to be safe. He took photos and a couple of casts."

"I should have more information about the brand of boot once the lab has processed everything," Houston said.

"I don't want you staying by yourself at that cabin until this is resolved," Jake said.

"I have seven dogs," I reminded him. "I'll be fine."

Houston said, "Seven dogs aren't going to protect you from a guy with a gun."

"And neither will a roommate," I argued. "I have animals to take care of. I'm not leaving my cabin."

"I'll stay with her," Landon offered.

Everyone, including me, appeared to be surprised by that. "You'd be willing to stay out at my place?"

Landon shrugged. "Sure. Why not? You have a guest room, and we'd all feel better if you weren't alone."

"I'd welcome the company if you're serious, but I'm a lot better with a gun than you are, so I'm not sure how much protection you'll be."

"So you can protect me. I'll bring my stuff by later."

With that settled, the discussion went back to the list we'd made. This was important and I wanted to pay attention, but I couldn't help but notice the way Jake had checked out. Sitka, who had been lying nearby with Yukon and Kojak, must have sensed his distress, because he got up and wandered over to where he was sitting. He put his head in Jake's lap, and he began to run his fingers through Sitka's hair in response, but from the look on his face, his mind was a million miles away. Not that I blamed him. The revelation that Val hadn't been alone when she died was huge. I was having a hard time coming to grips with it, and I'd had over twelve hours to get used to the idea.

"I get why these names are on the list," Landon was saying. "Everyone is known to one or more members of the team, and they were all around when Val was with us. But I don't think any of them would have intentionally sent a mountain down on anyone."

"I agree," Dani said. "These are our neighbors. People we go to community picnics with. People we stop to chat with when we run into them in town. I can't see any of them being the person we're looking for."

"I don't know them the way you do, but I understand what you're saying," Houston replied. "Still, someone did it. Someone called in a fake rescue report with the intention of killing one or all of the members of the team who responded. All we can do is make a list and then work to eliminate people from it until someone begins to stand out. If any of you have a better idea, I'm open to it."

No one responded. I was sure that while there wasn't anyone on the list we could believe would want us dead, someone did, and chances were, it *was* someone we stopped to chat with at the market.

Houston looked at me. "Any dreams, visions, intuitions since last night?"

I shook my head. "No. I didn't sleep much last night, so I couldn't have a dream. If I do make a connection of any kind, I'll let you know, but to be honest, I doubt I will. I think the only reason I connected last night was because I was searching for someone in trouble, and the man's pain was so intense, it came through."

"I can't claim to fully understand what you do and how you do it, but when we worked together last spring to track down the man who was killing people from his past, you seemed to have an intuition of how he felt and why he did it. Is that a normal response to connecting with the person you're looking for?"

"Not really. In fact, that was the first time it happened. A very disturbing first. Normally, I can only connect with a victim: the person I'm meant to help rescue. I don't know why I connected with the killer back then or last night."

"It sounds like your gift might be growing," Landon observed.

I huffed out a breath. "Maybe. Though sharing thoughts and memories with a person who has so much evil in their heart isn't a gift I'm interested in." I looked at Houston. "But if I do connect with him again, I'll be sure to let you know."

"Is there anything the rest of us can do to help with the investigation?" Sarge asked Houston. "I'd like to be involved, and I think the others would as well. When you lose one of your own, the urge to fight back is strong."

"Just talk to people. You've all lived here for a long time. That background is valuable. There's a good chance someone knows something, even if they don't realize it."

"What do you mean by that?" Dani looked unsure.

"I'm sorry to be confusing. What I mean is, in the course of going about their day, people observe and overhear thousands of pieces of data. If prompted, the individuals with whom you cross paths might remember something about you or vice versa. Oftentimes, a comment tossed out in a restaurant or an overheard telephone conversation can provide just the lead we need." Houston looked at the whiteboard on which we'd made the list. "I'll talk to these folks and track down and verify alibis, so we can pare down the list one at a time. If none of them pan out, we'll meet again to come up with another list. I can't say we'll be able to wrap this up quickly, but I'm committed to working on it for as long as it takes."

When the meeting broke up, Jake excused himself and headed toward his house, which was across the parking lot from the bar. Jordan followed. I hoped he'd be okay. He hadn't said much at all since I'd shared my news. Val's death had been such a dark time for both of us. I hated that we were being forced to relive it.

Dani announced that she had a charter that afternoon. People often hired her to fly them to remote locations to take photos of the wildlife that's so abundant in Alaska. She'd be out of cell range, but she had her radio and would check in with us when she got back.

Sarge headed to the kitchen for some cooking therapy. While Neverland was closed there wouldn't be any customers to feed whatever masterpiece he came up with, so I had a feeling if I stopped by later in the day I'd be treated to a feast worthy of a king.

Landon kissed my cheek and reminded me he'd come by my place later that afternoon with his things and left as well. He didn't say where he was going, but the serious expression on his face told me that he had an idea he intended to follow up on. He was by far the smartest member of the S&R team. Not only was he a genius by anyone's standards, he was a master hacker as well. I didn't think there was an internet site he couldn't hack in to, and his skill had come in handy on more than one occasion.

"I guess I'll get started on this list," Houston said as he motioned to Kojak that he was ready to leave. "Are you heading home?"

"No. At least not right away. I'm going to the shelter for a couple of hours. We've been really busy since the grand opening and fund-raiser last month. I think Harley plans to come in today, and I want to catch up with him before he goes back to Los Angeles."

"I thought he was going to be in town until after the holidays."

"He was. And he'll be back. He'll only be gone for a couple of weeks."

"And after the shelter?"

"After that, I'll probably head home." I met Houston's gaze. "You don't have to worry about me. I'll be fine."

"I know. You're very capable. I'm worried about everyone on the team."

"You think this guy might not be done?"

"The thought has occurred to me," Houston admitted. "Until we catch him, you all should be extra careful."

I nodded. "I'll be careful. If you get any leads, call me."

"I will. And if you have a vision, call me."

I picked up my bag and motioned to Yukon.

Houston put a hand on my shoulder as I turned to the door. "I know how hard this is, but I want you to know I'm going to get this guy."

"I know," I said. And I believed we would. The problem was, I couldn't be sure we were destined to track him down before he took another life.

Chapter 4

When I arrived at the Rescue Alaska Animal Shelter, I found one of our regular volunteers, Serena Walters, on duty. She was holding a puppy and talking to a woman in a brown coat when I walked in, so I waved to her and went back to the little office we used for administrative duties. I took off my jacket and hung it up on the coatrack. There was a pile of mail on the desk, which I picked up and began to thumb through.

"Who is this little guy?" I asked Serena, who was still holding the puppy, probably a mixed breed, when she joined me.

"This is Chester. The woman wants to surrender him to us. Her daughter got him from a woman who was giving away puppies in front of the grocery store, but she didn't have permission to bring home a pet, and she absolutely doesn't want to keep it."

I held out my arms and Serena passed him over. "He sure is a cute little thing. And of course we'll take him. He's better off with us than with someone who doesn't want him. Was the woman willing to leave her contact information?"

"No. She just handed me the pup, explained the situation, and left."

While we tried to get contact information for everyone who surrendered a pet, more often than not those dropping off animals weren't willing to take the time. "That's fine. Let's get him set up in one of the kennels. I'll run him over to Kelly," I said, referring to the local vet, "so she can give him his shots and a healthy puppy check. Have we had any other new arrivals since I was in on Friday?"

"No. The lady from the clinic, the tall one with the short red hair whose name escapes me, came in and picked up the poodle she filled out paperwork for. I had just left, but Trevor took care of it. Harley stopped in yesterday. He was sorry to have missed you but might be back today on his way out of town."

"I thought he wasn't leaving until tomorrow."

"He changed his flight and is leaving from Fairbanks this evening. Oh, and some guy was in looking for you this morning. He gave me an envelope to give to you."

I narrowed my gaze. "What guy? What envelope?"

Serena plucked an envelope from the bottom of the stack I was holding. "This envelope. As for the guy, I didn't recognize him. He was tall. Dark hair. Built."

I opened the envelope and found a photo of me standing next to Yukon. The photo had been taken on the mountain just minutes before the explosion. Given the angle of the photo, it looked to have been taken with a telephoto lens from above where I stood. "This guy—did he leave a name?"

Serena shook her head. "No. He just came in the front door and asked if you were here. When I said you weren't, he gave me the envelope and asked me to give it to you when I saw you."

There was nothing in the envelope other than the photo, but it might have prints or DNA on it that would help us identify the person who left it, so I set both on the desk and called Houston. He immediately said he was on his way over, and I wasn't to let Serena leave before he got there.

I hung up and turned back to Serena. "Did anyone else see the guy who left this?"

She shook her head. "No, just me. I was in the main lobby by myself when he came in. He handed me the envelope and left. What's going on?"

"Did you hear about our rescue last night?"

"I haven't heard a thing. Did something happen?"

I took a few minutes to fill her in, leaving out the parts I thought might be sensitive to the case. I wasn't sure how much Houston wanted us to share.

Serena's hand flew to her mouth. "Oh, Harmony, I'm so sorry. I didn't know Austin well, but I know all of you were tight. Who would do such a thing?"

"That's what we're trying to figure out."

She raised a brow. "Do you think the guy who dropped off the envelope had something to do with it?"

"Maybe. The photo is of me just minutes before the explosion. As far as I know, the only person on that mountain besides the rescue team was the killer."

Serena gasped. "You think the guy who was here this morning was the killer?"

"He very well might have been. Officer Houston is going to have some questions for you."

"Of course. I'll help in any way I can."

With Houston's help, Serena was able to provide a better description than she'd given me. The man was six feet three or four inches. He had dark hair that brushed his collar and wore dark glasses, so she couldn't see the color of his eyes. She remembered thin lips that were almost completely hidden beneath a thick beard and mustache. He was thin but built, muscular, like someone who lifted weights. Serena estimated he was probably between thirty and forty, although it was hard to tell with all the facial hair. He didn't have an accent exactly, but he tended to slur his Rs, and wore black boots, dark denim jeans, and a neutral-color sweatshirt; Serena thought beige. It seemed like a lot to go on, but between the beard and the dark glasses, it was hard to come up with a helpful image. I sorted through the details after Houston took them down, but not a single person who looked like that came to mind.

Houston wore gloves when he handled the photo and envelope, then put them in a plastic bag with the intention of forwarding it to the county lab.

"Do you think you can get DNA or a print?" I asked.

"Probably not, but we'll try. The flap of the envelope was folded in, not sealed, so we won't get DNA there. He may have left prints on the photo, but I'd be surprised if he handled it without wearing gloves. I'd say it was careless of him to come to the shelter looking for you. If he just wanted you to have the photo, he could have left it on your windshield or under the mat outside the door. Why would he show up personally when he had to know we're looking for him?"

"I can't think of a single reason unless he wants to get caught or he's cocky enough to think we couldn't catch up with him even if we figured out who he is."

"I'd say the guy who delivered the letter wasn't the killer, just someone who was given some cash to do it, but I'll have a sketch artist work on the description Serena gave me and follow any lead. If I can find the guy who made the delivery, he might be able to describe the person who gave him the envelope. Every lead is a worthwhile lead."

I leaned a hip against the desk. "Why did he have the photo delivered anyway? Is he threatening me? He obviously knows where I spend a significant amount of my time."

Houston frowned. "I wish I knew. It could be a threat of sorts, but," he pursed his lips and shook his head slowly, "it feels like something else is going on."

"I agree."

"I don't want you going off anywhere alone. I feel like if he just wanted you dead, he could easily have taken care of that last night. But he wants something, and that makes me very uncomfortable."

"I'll be careful," I promised. "After I leave here I'm going to the feedstore, then back to my cabin. Landon said he'd be there by this afternoon. I'll wait for him to show up before I walk the dogs. If the guy who came here today is one we're after, he made a mistake I plan to exploit. Landon is a genius on the computer. Once we have a sketch of him, Landon should be able to use his software to identify him."

"Good to know. The equipment in our lab is so outdated, it's pretty worthless. If Landon has updated equipment, I might work something out with him for casework. Maybe I'll pop by later to talk to him about it."

"Why don't you pick up some takeout when you get off, then come by my place? The three of us can work together."

******

The dogs were more than ready for their walk when Landon arrived, so I grabbed my rifle and the two of us set off with them. There was a heavy cloud cover, but other than a few flurries here and there, there wasn't a lot of moisture. The temperature drop the previous evening seemed to indicate we might be in for some snow, which was inevitable at this time of year.

"I've been thinking about things since we met this morning," Landon said as the dogs headed toward the property boundary where we often turned around. "I wasn't there last night, so my opinion is going to be slightly skewed, but it seems as if for this guy to have set the dynamite in the exact location required to create a landslide at the narrowest part of the gulch, he must have had experience doing it."

I picked up a stick and tossed it for Honey. "That makes sense. I don't know a thing about blowing things up, but there has to be a technique to it. A lot of people around here have experience with dynamite, though. Folks use it to blow stumps, it's used in the mines, it's sometimes used for landslide control and to break up ice. I see where you're going with your line of thought, but I'm not sure using possession of dynamite or knowing how to use it will serve as much of a way to narrow people down."

"Maybe you're right. I took a hike up to the spot where I estimated the charge would have to have been set. There's evidence someone was up there, but whoever set the charge went back to clean things up. There was a light snow on the mountain overnight too, which further masked whatever evidence would have been left behind. I found a couple of shell casings from a rifle near the point of the explosion. No one was shot, so I have no reason to believe they were left by the killer rather than someone who was up there some other time, but I brought them back just in case."

"Houston's coming by with dinner for the three of us when he gets off work. You can give them to him then."

Landon glanced in my direction. "Is there something going on between the two of you?"

"Not that it's any of your business, but we're just friends. The same way you and I are friends."

"Figured, but it seems like I find you together quite a bit lately."

"I've been helping him train Kojak. I'm not sure he's cut out for police work; maybe search and rescue someday. Even if that doesn't work out, he's good for PR. Houston takes him to work with him and folks seem to love him."

"And Harley?"

I frowned. "Harley likes Kojak just fine, but that's an odd question."

Landon chuckled. "What I meant is, are you and Harley dating?"

"Again, none of your business, but again, no. What is it with all these questions?"

Landon shrugged. "Just curious. We haven't had a lot of opportunity to hang out lately and I feel sort of out of the loop."

I laced my fingers through Landon's. "It *has* been a while since we've hung out and just chatted. I hate the reason you feel the need to babysit me, but this is nice. When Wyatt's released from the hospital, the three of us should get together for a movie marathon. We haven't done that since last fall, when we all hung out at my cabin for a horror fest."

"We should plan on it again this Halloween." Landon paused. "Do you think we should call the dogs back? It looks like the clouds are about to open up."

"Yeah, we should head back. I still have to clean the barn and the cat boxes." I let out a loud whistle to call the dogs, who were walking ahead of us. They all came back right away except for Denali, Mr. Independent. The big guy had a mind of his own.

"Denali," I called as loudly as I could shout.

My call was met with rapid barking.

I glanced at Landon. "Wait here with the others. I'll get him."

I told the other dogs to stay, then jogged forward. When I got to the end of the clearing where I'd found the footprints that morning, I found Denali staring intently into the thick brush. "What do you see?"

Denali growled.

I didn't see anything, but I wasn't comfortable with the situation. "Come on. Let's go home."

Denali let out five barks in rapid succession, then turned and followed me. I wasn't sure what he'd seen or smelled, but I didn't want whatever—or whoever—it was hanging around so close to my cabin.

"Everything okay?" Landon asked.

"Something just spooked Denali. It happens. Let's head back so I can get my chores done before Houston shows up."

"You realize you shouldn't have taken off like that by yourself, right?"

I smiled. "I know I promised to protect you, but I did leave you with six dogs."

"That's not what I meant."

"I know. Stop worrying. I'll be fine."

Even as I said the words, I knew deep in my gut that no matter how much I wanted them to be true, it didn't seem as if things were going to be fine at all.

Chapter 5

By the time Houston arrived with the food, Landon and I had cleaned the barn, tidied up the cat boxes, fed everyone, and even straightened up the cabin. Because Neverland was closed, Houston had brought dinner from the inn, which was a nice change of pace even though I adored Sarge's cooking.

"Please tell me you've managed to whittle down the list we created this morning," I jumped right in once we'd all served ourselves and sat down at the dining table. "Not that I think any of the twenty guys we came up with is our man, but it's a good idea to definitively eliminate them."

"I have the list of more than twenty down to four," Houston informed me. "I don't necessarily suspect any of them, but I was unable to speak to them to verify alibis, so they stay on the list. The others all provided verifiable alibis."

"Who are the four left?" I asked.

"Vance Tisdale, Grange Littleman, Paul Gentry, and Kent Paulson."

All four of them had lived and worked in Rescue since before Val's death. All were tall men—over six feet—and had dark hair. I didn't believe any of them were capable of murder, but if you loosely interpreted facial and body features, any of them could have given Serena the photo of me, though none had a beard unless they'd grown one since I'd last seen them. Of course, all were probably known to her.

"Serena knows all of them, I think, so they couldn't have delivered the photo to the shelter, but we've already acknowledged that the killer could have had someone else do that. All four men are tall, so they'd likely wear a size twelve boot or larger. Did you verify the footprints behind my cabin were from a size twelve boot?"

"I did," Houston said.

"Here's what I don't get: Why would this guy have someone deliver the photo to Harmony at the shelter?" Landon asked. "If he wanted to scare her, why not e-mail it to her? Or text it to her if he didn't have her e-mail address? Why the personal touch provided by hand delivery, especially if he used a proxy?"

"Good question," Houston said. "If he'd delivered the envelope personally, I'd say he hoped she'd open it right away and he could enjoy the look of fear in her eyes. But if he had someone else make the delivery, it does seem an electronic delivery would have been more efficient."

I leaned back in my chair. "I know we need to look at everyone, but I don't think any of the four men is the sort to kill a person who's just trying to help."

"Maybe not, but someone set off that charge. Tell me a little bit about each man," Houston suggested.

I took a sip of my coffee as I considered what I knew about them. "Vance Tisdale owns a local cabinet shop. He's married with three children. He was probably put on the list because he was the subject of a rescue two winters ago. He'd gone ice climbing and had a fall, and a team had to go out to get him. I think he was grateful for the assist, and as far as I know, he didn't have any bad feelings about it. I can't see why he'd want to kill anyone."

"Would you say he'd know how to use dynamite with the sort of precision needed to cause a controlled landslide?"

"Yes. His business can be sporadic, so he supplements it by working for road crews. He'd have had training in the use of explosives to create controlled landslides."

Houston jotted down a few notes. "Go on."

"Grange Littleman tends bar at a place on the highway called Shooters. He's the sort who likes to hunt and fish. I imagine he's probably handled dynamite from time to time. As far as I know, he's never been the subject of a rescue, but he sometimes hangs out with Wyatt. They're both single and about the same age."

"And Paul Gentry?" Houston asked.

"Never married. No children. Works construction in the summer and sells firewood in the winter. He also helps out with road crew. He's the shortest and heaviest of the four. As far as I know, he's never been involved in a rescue."

"Paul hasn't, but he was good friends with Trace Colton," Landon pointed out. "Trace died up on the mountain maybe ten years ago," he informed Houston. "Maybe it was even farther back than that."

I frowned. "It was fourteen years ago, and it was the same mountain as the call came in for last night." I looked at Houston. "I remember the rescue clearly. Trace and Paul were just kids. Actually, teenagers, around my age. They'd gone hiking and the weather turned bad. They got disoriented in the snow and Trace fell. He was hurt pretty bad. Paul tried to help him, but Trace was gone by the time Val and Jake got to him."

"So, maybe he blames the team for not getting to Trace in time to save him," Houston said.

"Maybe," I agreed.

"Seems like a real suspect," Houston said. He took a minute to make more notes. "What about Kent Paulson?"

"Kent is widowed," I answered. "He has two children, a boy and a girl, both young. He sells insurance. As far as I know, he's never been directly involved in a rescue, although his home burned to the ground at about this time last year. His wife didn't make it out. Kent was very vocal in placing the blame for his wife's death on the volunteer firefighters. He felt they took too long to respond."

"So he might hold a grudge against first responders in general," Houston said.

"I guess," I said. "I'd say he's a good candidate, but my vision of Val through the man's eyes doesn't fit him. Kent would have been a kid when Val died. I don't think it could have been him. It would have to be someone who had the ability and opportunity to be up on the mountain during that storm."

Houston tapped his pen on his little notebook. "So, of the four, you think Paul Gentry is the best candidate?"

I nodded. "I'm not saying it was him—personally, I don't think it was—but if I had to choose one of the four, it would be him."

Houston clicked his pen shut and put it in his shirt pocket, then added his little notebook. "I plan to talk with all four men tomorrow, providing I can track them down. If they have alibis, I move on. If one or more don't have alibis, I'll take a closer look. I suspect the team might have other names to suggest by then. We could meet again tomorrow if we have something to discuss. It would help if one of you could call the others to ask them if they have names to add to the list."

"I'll do it," I offered.

"I'll poke around on the internet to see if I can come up with anything," Landon added. "I think it's relevant that the man who blew up the mountain thought of Val just as it went. It's been thirteen years, though, so if there's a link, why now? I'm hoping if I dig deep enough, I can find a link between something that happened at around that time and something that's happened recently."

I rested my elbows on the table, then put my head in my hands. It seemed so surreal to be dealing with Val's death again thirteen years after the fact. I kept seeing her lying on the dirt floor of that cave through the eyes of the man who very well might have killed her. I tried to remember what he was feeling as he reviewed that memory, but all I could get back to was his rage as he put into action something that would lead to the loss of a man's life.

I felt a hand on my shoulder. "Are you okay?" Houston asked.

I nodded and then lifted my head. "I'm fine. Just tired. I didn't sleep last night. I'm sure I'll crash early this evening." I stood up and looked around for a way to change the subject. I needed time with my thoughts before I was ready to discuss them. "I have ice cream if anyone's interested." I took several steps toward the kitchen with a stack of plates from the table. Not the best segue, I realized, but it seemed to do the job because Landon and Houston began gathering dishes too. I opened the freezer and was reaching for the ice cream when my phone rang.

"Hello," I answered.

"Lumber over to the yard for the next kaboom."

I looked at my phone after the person on the other end hung up. "I think that was him. He said to *lumber over to the yard for the next kaboom.*"

Houston stood up. "Did he say where?"

I ran out the back door without answering. Was he going to blow up something in my yard? I looked toward my newly rebuilt barn, then at the dogs, who were watching me but didn't seem concerned. No, this wasn't the yard he'd meant.

"Harm?" Houston put a hand on my arm. "Did he say where?"

"No. That was the entire message." I frowned. "But the phrase seemed specific. *Lumber over to the yard.*" I looked at Houston. "The lumber mill."

Houston ran toward his truck. He called the county dispatch and learned there'd been a fire reported at the local lumber mill. "I think you're right. I need to go."

"We're coming with you." I called the dogs into the cabin, then Landon and I grabbed our jackets and joined Houston at his truck.

"We need to call the volunteer firefighters to warn them," I said.

"The number for the county dispatch is the one I just called from my phone." Houston handed it to me.

I hit Redial and waited, but the line went dead instead of ringing through. I tried again with the same result. "We must be in a dead zone. The cell reception is really bad out here."

Houston picked up his radio and tried to call the county sheriff, but all we could hear was static. "That's odd," Houston said. "Bad cell reception shouldn't affect the radio."

"Maybe someone tampered with it," Landon suggested.

The idea seemed unlikely, but with everything that was going on, I supposed it was possible.

"Or," Landon said, "maybe someone is using something that's interfering with the signal."

That, I admitted, could be it.

By the time we arrived at the lumber mill, the place was fully enflamed. I looked at the group of men fighting the fire and gasped. "My God. Get them to move back."

The minute the words left my mouth, the entire building exploded in a flash of white light. It happened so fast, I barely had the chance to breathe, let alone react. After a moment, Houston, Landon, and I all jumped from the vehicle and ran toward the victims.

Four men were down. We began checking for pulses. Three of the men had suffered from cuts and burns but were still alive. The last man, though, the one who'd been closest to the mill when it exploded, never had a chance. I put a hand to my mouth, closed my eyes, and swallowed hard. I said a quick prayer for him, then turned to Houston. "Do you have a blanket?"

"In the cargo area of the truck. And there's a metal box in the shell with supplies. Grab the first aid kit too. The shell isn't locked."

I tried to quell my nausea as I ran back to the truck. I wanted to fall to my knees and weep, but there was work to be done, so I grabbed the blanket and went back to cover the body. Then I called Jake and told him to deploy the team and have Dani on standby for an air evac to the hospital in Fairbanks. Two air evacs in two nights must be a record.

I started to walk to where Houston was talking to one of the men who'd survived when I had the distinct sensation someone was watching me. I paused and looked around but didn't see anyone. It was probably just my nerves getting the best of me. I didn't have time for a breakdown. I had work to do. There were three survivors and three of us, so we'd each take one to comfort until medical help arrived.

"What are we going to do about the fire?" I asked Houston as I worked to apply a compress to the forehead of the man I was working on. The mill was burning uncontrollably, threatening the piles of logs waiting to be milled and the forest beyond the property.

Houston looked at the fire truck, which wasn't being manned. "I'll see if I can get some water on it.

When Jake gets here, tell him to round up whoever he can find to help."

The next few hours were a blur. Somehow, we got the three survivors stabilized and Jordan and Dani took off to the hospital in Fairbanks with them. Jake managed to round up enough help from the locals, many of whom had come out as soon as the explosion alerted them to the problem, to get the fire under control. The mill was a total loss, but the piles of lumber and, more importantly, the forest beyond was saved.

The man who'd died had been taken to the morgue, and Houston had notified his wife and teenage children. Of all the jobs that had to be dealt with in an emergency, that was the one I least wanted to do. I couldn't imagine being able to find the words I'd need. I didn't think I could watch the light die from the eyes of the surviving family, knowing their life would never be the same again.

When Landon and I got back to my cabin I felt as if I'd been to hell and back. All I wanted to do was take a shower to wash off the smoke and blood and then fall into bed. As we'd approached the front door after Jake dropped us off, I noticed something was taped to the front door. It was a photo of me, standing with my head turned as the fire raged behind me.

"I remember this," I said quietly. "I felt like someone was watching me, so I looked around."

"But you didn't see anyone?"

I shook my head. "No. I decided it was just nerves and went back to work." I felt a lump form in my throat. "He was there watching. Just like last night. The death and destruction brought him joy." I willed my heart to slow. "No, not joy. Release."

"Release?"

I looked directly at Landon. "Emotional release. He finds solace in causing pain to others."

Chapter 6

Monday, October 15

Jake called me the next morning to let me know he'd spoken to Houston. They'd agreed that gathering all the first responders in town to the table for a debriefing and strategy session was a must. Houston had two full-time officers working under him, and there were seven members of the volunteer fire department who were well enough to attend. Additionally, there were six of us from the search-and-rescue team if you counted Sarge. Neverland was still closed, so everyone was told to meet at the bar at two o'clock.

"I have to hand it to this guy," Landon said as we walked my dogs. "Not only has he managed to kill two men and injure a handful of others, but given his history of targeting members of the community who've pledged to protect and serve, he's crippling the town as a whole."

"What do you mean?" I asked as Honey trotted a few feet ahead in search of a stick.

"What do you think is going to happen the next time someone gets lost, or a stray spark starts a fire? Everyone will be terrified. I wouldn't be a bit surprised if folks didn't refuse to respond to any emergency until this guy is caught."

Landon had a point. The deaths of two members of our community was going to be at the forefront of everyone's mind if and when another call came in. "The only way we're going to be able to alleviate the fear is to find him and put him behind bars. I know it seems as if we don't have any real clues yet, but I think the one we do have is an important one."

"The memory of Val's death?"

I nodded. "Val's body was found in a cave high up on the mountain. For the killer to have a memory of her death, he had to have been there. Given the terrain and the storm, I'd say there were only a limited number of people who could have been there. Anyone younger than, say, fifteen at the time most likely wouldn't have been out in the storm, and anyone over the age of around sixty-five most likely wouldn't have had the stamina to make the trip under those circumstances."

"That's still a lot of people."

I shrugged. "Maybe. But if you factor in that the killer was in the area thirteen years ago and now, it narrows things down a bit. Rescue isn't the sort of place where a lot of people stick. Most folks who come here experience their first endless winter and leave before the next."

"True."

"I also have the feeling this guy knew Val, although the grief he felt when she died might have been tied to some other memory her death brought forth. But if he did know her, I don't know how, or how well. Still, I won't be surprised if we find out that he'd at least met her before that night on the mountain."

"The fact that he's targeting first responders does make it seem as if he might have had a bad experience with them. He might have lost someone because the S&R team didn't find them in time, or maybe he lost someone in a fire." Landon reached down and scratched Lucky on the head when we paused so I could toss a stick for Honey. "I'll log on to my laptop when we get back to your place. Houston planned to talk to the last four people on the list this morning, but maybe we can come up with a new one before the meeting in case none of them pan out."

"Okay. I'll help. We were both around when Val died. It could be beneficial to compare memories." I tossed the stick, then started walking again, cradling my rifle to my chest all the while. "I spent some time in the middle of the night thinking about the fact that this guy seems to be focusing on me. As far as I know, he hasn't sent photos to Jake, and he and I were both there for the first explosion." I paused and mulled the idea. "That feels intentional, but I don't see how it could be. Even if he called in the fake rescue, as we suspect, he couldn't have known who would respond. And while he called me last night, he couldn't have known I'd call Jake."

"You could be the target or the trigger or something. I want you to be extra careful."

"I will. Let's see what we can dig up before we need to leave for Neverland."

******

Back at the cabin, Landon logged on to the computer and I went into the barn to check on Homer and the rabbits. Kodi and Juno were tired after their walk, so I gave them fresh food and water, which they'd enjoy before settling in for their midmorning nap. Homer couldn't see me, but he heard me and always seemed to enjoy listening to my voice, so I chatted while I cleaned out his stall and refreshed his food and water. Until a few weeks ago, Homer had had a roommate, a baby moose named Rocky, who'd been accepted by a moose rescue and transferred to a more permanent situation.

Before leaving the barn, I fed and watered the rabbits as well. Taking care of my menagerie was expensive and time consuming, but it provided me with a feeling of contentment and satisfaction. Living alone in the middle of nowhere, they were also good company.

"Have you found anything?" I asked Landon after pouring myself a cup of coffee.

"Not exactly, but I did have an idea." He stopped what he was doing and looked over at me. "After every rescue since I've been part of the team, Jake has done a debriefing. He keeps a log of who the rescue subject was, who responded, the date, time of day, weather conditions, and any special circumstances."

"I know. I'm part of the team too."

"My point is that, given our theory that the killer might have been on the receiving end of a botched rescue, I thought it might be a valuable exercise to go back through the logs to look at the rescues recorded during the year before Val's death. Maybe he knew her because she was a member of the team when the instigating event occurred."

I sat back, considering. It sounded as if it would take a lot of time, but something might pop out that seemed relevant. "I guess that seems like a good idea. Have all the old logs been computerized?"

"Yes. Jake keeps a hard copy, but I transcribe everything into an online database after each debriefing. If you want to get your laptop, we can divide the entries. If either of us sees anything we think might mean something, we'll stop to discuss it."

I went into my bedroom and grabbed my laptop. I'd just returned to the living area when my phone rang.

It was Houston. "Hey. What's up?" I asked.

"I'm just checking in on you," Houston said. "The fire was pretty horrific, and you went through something equally terrible the night before, so I wanted to make sure you were okay."

"I'm fine," I informed Houston. "Don't get me wrong, I wish none of this was happening, but I've got a thick hide so there's no reason to worry about me."

Houston chuckled. "I guess I shouldn't have worried. Is Landon still with you?"

"Like glue on a glitter board. We're going back through the debriefing notes from the year before Val died. I still think it's relevant that the thought in the guy's head the moment he sent the mountain down on team members was Val's death."

"I agree. And going back through the logs is an excellent idea."

"How did your interviews go?"

"I managed to speak to all but one of the men. It looks like Grange Littleman, Kent Paulson, and Vance Tisdale all have alibis for the time of the landslide. I haven't managed to track down Paul Gentry, but I'll keep trying."

"The more I think about it, Paul seems like a real suspect. I'd forgotten what happened with his friend Trace until Landon mentioned it last night."

"You said Paul works construction in the summer and sells firewood in the winter. What would he be doing at this time of year?"

"Probably cutting, splitting, and stacking firewood. Have you checked his house? He should be there."

"I've called him and checked his house. He isn't answering his phone or his door. I spoke to the neighbor who lives closest to him, and he said he hadn't seen Paul for a few days at least. I asked if that was odd, and he said Paul likes to go hunting."

"It *is* hunting season, and if Paul was off the grid, his phone wouldn't work. Landon and I hope to have some names to add to your list by the time we see you this afternoon."

"Okay."

I hung up and returned my attention to Landon. "I guess you heard."

Landon nodded.

"So we're down to just Paul. It could be him, but it just as likely isn't. Have you found anything yet?"

"I flagged two rescues I'd like to discuss. It might help to have Jake here for it, though."

I took my phone back out. "I'll call him."

We wanted to wait for Jake before we began our discussion, so I made some sandwiches while Landon continued his search. In a way, it felt like we were grasping at straws. We could only speculate at the reason the man who had set off two explosions and killed two men was doing it. For all we really knew, he just liked to blow stuff up.

And then I remembered the intense pain I'd felt the night of the landslide. No, the things he was doing were intentional, not random at all.

By the time Jake had arrived with Sitka, Landon had gone through half the rescues in the year before Val died and flagged three. I was still a teen then and not an official member of the team, but I hung around the bar a lot when I wasn't in school, and I manned the radio from time to time. Jake would have clearer memories of the rescues, but I might have something to add.

"The first one I flagged was the fraternity rescue," Landon began.

"That was the one when that group of college kids went backcountry skiing just before Thanksgiving," Jake said. "They got lost, and three of the six ended up dead from exposure."

"That's right," Landon verified. "I flagged this one for two reasons. First, there were both survivors and nonsurvivors involved, and if I remember correctly, the survivors had been through a lot by the time they were found and airlifted out. And second, the rescue occurred just a month before Val's death."

"I don't remember any of those kids as being from around here," I said.

"They weren't. In fact, they were all from the lower forty-eight. But we don't definitively know the killer has been in Rescue this whole time. If your vision is accurate, he was up on the mountain the day Val died and again when he caused the landslide. We can't say where he's been between the two events."

Jake drummed his fingers on the table. "Okay. That's a fair statement. And I do remember that rescue. The kids who survived were in bad shape. I think one of them lost a foot to frostbite, and another was so far gone he was completely delirious. He kept talking about someone named Zane being bitten by zombies. The thing is, there wasn't anyone named Zane in the group."

"You checked with the others to verify that?"

"I did. The others said there'd only been six of them, the three we rescued and the three whose bodies we found."

"Another aspect of this rescue is that the father of one of the boys who died blamed the S&R team for not finding the kids in a timely manner," Landon added. "In fact, at one point I think he was talking about filing a lawsuit against them."

"That's true," Jake verified. "The case never went anywhere. The father was grieving deeply, but the kids were caught in a blizzard and weren't at all equipped to wait it out. The team showed up and was ready to move out as soon as the storm let up a bit, but it took more than twenty-four hours from the time of the rescue request until it was safe to go in. Even then, it really wasn't safe, but with the experienced people we had, it was doable."

"Who was involved in the rescue?" I asked Landon.

Landon looked at the computer. "Jake, Val, Devon, and Dani."

Devon had been Dani's boyfriend at the time, a visitor to the area she'd met over the summer. He'd decided to stick around for a while and Dani had lived with him for a while, but he'd eventually left when she decided it was time for her to move out and move on. The breakup had been messy, and as far as I knew, Devon had never returned to Rescue.

"I think this rescue might be relevant. Let's print out the details and we can talk about it at the meeting later," I suggested.

"Okay. What else do you have flagged?" Jake asked.

"Nicky Nolan." Landon looked up. "Nicky was a local kid. It says here he was twenty when he went hiking with his girlfriend, Charisse Cole. The couple ran into a grizzly while hiking the river trail in late fall, and Charisse was attacked and killed. Nicky hid in a small space provided by a rock outcropping. He was terrified to come out even after the bear left, so he hadn't made it home. His dad sent the team out looking for him. They found what was left of Charisse's body first, then later noticed Nicky cowering in his hiding place."

"The kid was a mess." Jake shook his head. "I guess I'd be a mess too if I'd seen my girlfriend mauled to death. Nicky's family lived in town for another decade, but as far as I know, Nicky never came back after he left for college a few weeks after the incident."

"Why did you flag this one?" I asked Landon. "It doesn't sound as if Nicky was even in Alaska when Val died."

"It's true there isn't any evidence he came back once he left, but the violence of the whole thing spoke to me." Landon crossed his arms over his chest. "I guess the guy wouldn't have a reason to hold a grudge against the S&R team. I'll go ahead and unflag this one. Which just leaves a note relating to the team who was trapped in the fire the summer before Val died."

"I remember that," I said. "It was awful." I shuddered when I remembered the church group that had gone hiking in the canyon during a hot stretch. A fire broke out and trapped them. There were twelve kids and four adults all told, and only seven of the kids and one of the adults made it out alive.

Jake nodded. "It really was a tragedy."

"While I don't see how that incident could relate to Val's death, the survivors could on some level blame the fact that the S&R team couldn't get to them before the deaths of their friends. Given what happened last night, I suppose we should consider it an important side note that fire was involved. I think we should print this one off as well."

Jake's phone rang just as Landon hit the Print button. Jake hadn't said as much, at least not yet, but based on his side of the conversation and the look on his face, the team had just been called in on a rescue. My heart started to pound; I had to wonder whether this one was real or if it was another trap.

Chapter 7

The frantic parents of a two-year-old boy paced in the background as Jake brought the team up to speed. "Georgie Baker was last seen watching cartoons in the living room of the home his parents rented for their autumn vacation," Jake began as the entire team, including the dogs, stood in the driveway in front of a small house on the river. "His parents were in the kitchen sharing a pot of coffee and discussing their plans for the day when Mrs. Baker went to check on Georgie. In the living room she found the television on and the Bakers' dog asleep in front of the fire, but the room was otherwise empty. The Bakers have searched the house from top to bottom and the area surrounding the home to no avail. It's their opinion that Georgie wouldn't cross the road. He's been forbidden to do so and seems to understand the consequences. That means he most likely followed the river in one direction or the other, and then possibly veered off from there. We'll divide into two teams. One will head upriver, the other down. Harmony, Landon, and Dani, take Yukon and head upstream. Jordan, Sitka, and I will go downstream. Any questions?"

"What was he wearing?" Dani asked.

"Good question. When last seen, Georgie had on a pair of blue jeans and a gray flannel shirt. He wore a pair of fuzzy Cookie Monster slippers on his feet." Jake held up two plastic bags, each with a T-shirt inside. He handed one to me. The T-shirts would be used to provide Georgie's scent to the dogs.

"Are the police involved in the search?" Landon asked.

"Officer Houston was responding to a home invasion by a hungry bear when the call came in. He'll be here as soon as the bear's been removed. His officers are coming out to help as well. We were the first to respond, so we'll get started."

"Be sure your radios are on channel two," Sarge, who had arrived to man the radio, reminded us. "Things are tense given what's been going on, but it's our job to find this boy, so let's head out and bring him home."

"Have you tried to make a connection?" Jordan asked me before we separated.

"I tried when we first arrived but didn't pick up anything. I'll keep at it as we make our way upstream. If I get a vision, I'll let you know."

As my team started out, I took the little T-shirt out of the bag and let Yukon take a good long sniff. "This is Georgie. Find Georgie."

Yukon set off down the narrow trail that skirted the river. The portion was closest to the house wound its way through a wide-open meadow, but I could see the forest was dense up ahead. As I considered heading into a closed-in, darker place, the trepidation I'd been experiencing since we'd received the call increased dramatically.

"Is anyone else totally freaked out right now?" Dani, who was usually never bothered by anything, asked.

"It is a little nerve-racking," I answered. "But unlike the rescue on Friday, we were able to interview the people who called in the rescue."

"And the parents did seem genuinely upset," Landon added. "I doubt they're faking the disappearance of their child just to get us out here."

"I guess," Dani said as she picked her way through a low spot that was sticky with black mud.

I paused to look for the tiny footprints that would have been made by a two-year-old's slippers but didn't find any, so I once again instructed Yukon to find Georgie and followed him.

"What if this guy kidnapped the kid to force the rescue?" Dani said.

"Seems like a lot of trouble to go to," Landon countered.

"Maybe, but no one in this town is going to be very willing to respond to an emergency call of any kind now. Using a two-year-old would be smart. Who's going to refuse to look for a kid that young?"

Dani was right. If the killer had planned this rescue, he'd done a good job anticipating what it would take to get us out here.

"Hang on," I said as I stopped walking. "Let me try to make contact again. The kid couldn't have wandered too far away."

I called Yukon over to my side, then sat down on a large rock. I closed my eyes and focused on the image of the boy whose photo we'd been shown. Thick, straight blond hair. Bright blue eyes peeking out from behind long bangs. I had a clear image of the boy in my mind, but I couldn't *see* him and I didn't sense fear or distress. I was trying to go deeper when I heard the snap of a twig from behind me. I opened my eyes and jumped up. I whirled around but didn't see anything.

"I heard it too," Dani said. "Might have been a bear."

I knew we were both thinking of the *or* that could conclude that sentence. *It might have been a bear* or *a madman out to kill us.*

"Let's keep going," Landon suggested. "The sooner we find this kid, the better for everyone."

I took out the T-shirt again and gave Yukon another sniff. "This is Georgie. Find Georgie."

Yukon sniffed it, then took off. After a few more minutes, Landon spoke. "I don't think this is right. The missing kid is two. We must have walked over a quarter of a mile. I don't think he'd have traveled that far."

I took a breath and let it out. "I agree. Maybe we should…" My sentence was cut off when Yukon stopped and began to growl. I told him to stay, then clipped the leash into place. I wasn't sure what he sensed, but he wouldn't be growling at a two-year-old. It had to be someone or something else.

"Hold him." I gave the leash to Dani. "Call Jake to let him know what's going on."

"I'm coming with you," Landon said as we both inched forward. I could hear talking in the distance that sounded like a little kid. I looked at Landon, he nodded, and we continued. It only took a few minutes before the forest opened up and the boy came into view.

"Holy crap," I whispered.

"Holy crap is right," Landon seconded.

Georgie was sitting on the ground near the river, playing with a bear cub.

"What are we going to do?" Landon asked.

"We need to get him." I looked around. I didn't see the mama bear, but she had to be close by. In fact, the snapping twigs we'd heard must have been her. I raised the radio to my lips. "Harmony to Jake."

"Go for Jake."

"We found Georgie. He's sitting on the ground maybe fifty yards in front of us playing with a bear cub."

My announcement was met with dead silence. "A bear cub?" Jake eventually replied.

"A small one. Really small for this time of the year. It must have been the product of a late birth, probably a multiple birth, to be so small this late in the season."

"And the mom?"

"I don't see her, but mama bears don't usually wander too far from their cubs." I took a deep breath and looked at Landon, who was frowning. "What should we do?"

"One of you should approach slowly. Try to get Georgie to come to you, but keep your eyes open and be careful."

"I'll do it," Landon said.

"No, I will. Georgie might be less apt to be scared by a strange woman than he would by a strange man.

Warn Dani so she knows to watch out for mama and to keep Yukon quiet."

I focused my eyes on Georgie, then took a step forward. I said a little prayer, then took another step. I couldn't help but remember Charisse Cole's death by mauling as I slowly walked forward with my senses on full alert. If the mama bear was nearby—and I suspected she was—and considered us a threat to her baby—which I was certain she would—we'd all be in trouble. "Georgie," I called softly as I approached.

Georgie looked up at me. I must have scared him because he looked like he was about to start screaming bloody murder. I held up his shirt. "Your mama sent me. She thought you might be cold and would need a warm shirt to wear."

"Mama."

"That's right, Mama. I'm going to help you with your shirt, but you need to walk slowly toward me."

The boy stood up. His clothes were filthy. I supposed playing in the mud along the shoreline had provided enough of a distraction that he hadn't even known he was lost. Georgie pointed to the bear cub. "Doggy."

"Yes, but the doggy needs to go home to his mommy, just like you need to go home to yours. I need you to come slowly to me. Okay? Don't run. Just walk nice and slow."

Georgie did as I said. There was still no sign of mama bear, which was really odd unless she was dead. Once Georgie was safe, I'd work on rescuing the cub, but until Georgie was out of harm's way, I had to assume the mother bear was a threat.

Once I had Georgie, I began to slowly walk back to where we'd left Dani with Yukon. As soon as

Yukon came into view, Georgie did scream to be let down to play with the doggy. I set him down next to Dani.

"Okay, that was intense," Landon said.

"It was." I looked around. "But while I'm thrilled the mama didn't show up, I'm worried the mama didn't show up. I need to go back to make sure the baby is going to be okay."

"Are you nuts?" Dani asked. "What we need to do is to get out of here."

I looked at Landon.

"Let's ask Jake," he suggested.

I radioed Jake, who said he and Jordan were on their way, and that Houston had arrived with his deputies. Jake suggested I wait until they arrived before I went back to check on the cub. When they did, Houston had a tranquilizer gun in his hand, while the others, Carl and Donny, had rifles. Dani and Landon headed back to the house with Jordan and Georgie, and Jake and I walked on either side of Houston and a bit in front of the two men with guns. When we reached the spot where I'd seen the cub, he was gone. But there was blood. A lot of it. My stomach lurched as I considered all the possible reasons we'd find so much blood along the riverbank.

"It trails off to the rock outcropping over there." Jake pointed.

I nodded and followed as he stepped carefully forward.

"Are you sure about this?" Carl asked. "After everything that's happened, maybe we should leave well enough alone and go back."

"Yeah," Donny added. "We got the kid. Why risk it?"

75

Jake stopped walking. He looked at me.

"But the baby. If his mama is dead and we don't rescue him, he'll die."

"Better him than me," Carl said.

I huffed out a breath. "You don't have to come. Wait here. I'll go see what's going on."

Houston held out his hand. "Carl, give me your gun."

He frowned but didn't argue. Houston handed Carl's gun to Jake. "The two of you go back to the house," he said to the deputies. "We'll be along shortly."

I smiled at Houston as he turned once again toward the trail of blood. "I'm going to take the lead," Houston said. "Harm, you fall in behind me, and Jake, you take up the rear."

We proceeded at a pace that was slow enough to make my skin itch. I knew it was smart to take our time. I tried to focus on the environment. I'd sensed the killer before. If he was in the area, I hoped I'd sense him this time as well. I supposed the fact that I found myself hoping the biggest threat to our safety was going to be from a bear should have served as a clue that maybe this wasn't the best thing to do after all.

When we'd traveled most of the way to the rock structure, Houston stopped walking. "The blood gets heavier here."

I jumped when the shrubs rustled next to where I was standing. I swear, I had a full-on heart attack before I realized the rustling had come from the cub. I knelt down and offered a hand. "Where's your mama, sweetie?"

The cub let out a loud cry. I stood back up and looked around. If the mama was around, she would have heard that and most likely come running. The fact that we hadn't all been mauled to death yet seemed to indicate that the mama probably really was dead.

"Wait here," Houston said. "I'm going to see what's behind those rocks."

"It might be a trap," Jake cautioned.

"I'll take it slow and be careful. If I'm not back in a couple of minutes, send in the cavalry."

I held my breath as Houston stepped out of view. I counted each heartbeat as I waited. I half-expected there to be an explosion, but a couple of minutes later, Houston came back into view. "The mother bear's been shot," he informed us. "She isn't dead yet, but she's lost a lot of blood and is unconscious."

I remembered the rustling we'd heard and the snapping twigs in the forest. I'd thought it might have been a bear, but now I wondered if it hadn't been a hunter. "We need to get her to Kelly."

"She has to weigh a couple hundred pounds," Houston pointed out. "We'll never be able to carry her out of here."

Jake looked around. "I can make it back here in my truck. I'll need to wind my way through the areas of densest forest, but I can make it. You two can wait here and I'll get the truck and return for the mama. If she's still alive when I get back, we'll take her to Kelly. Either way, we'll take the cub with us."

******

Luck must have been on our side today because not only did we find Georgie unharmed and unafraid but we'd rescued the baby bear and gotten his mama to the veterinarian in time for her to at least have a small chance of recovery. For the time being, the baby bear would bunk in my barn in the stall that had previously been occupied by Rocky. Houston bought him a huge stuffed bear to snuggle with that was almost as big as his mama, Landon pitched in and bought a heated sleeping pad, and Jake hooked up the feeding machine he'd installed for Rocky when we rebuilt the barn after it had burned down. I thought the pen we'd put together for Grizwald—Griz for short, even though he was a black bear and not a grizzly—was warm and comfy, but when we put him inside, he stood in the middle of the pen and cried. I put my hand on my chest. My heart was breaking.

"He's scared," Jake said.

"And lonely," Houston added.

"Maybe I should have him sleep in the house. I have room in my bedroom for another dog bed. He's so small, he won't take up much room."

"I think that's a bad idea," Landon said. "He might be here awhile. Probably for the winter at least, if his mama dies. He's going to get bigger."

As we stood around debating what to do, Honey came into the barn. She took one look at the baby bear, walked into the stall, and started licking his face. He immediately stopped crying. Honey walked over to the heated sleeping pad and stretched out. Griz wandered over, curled up with her, and went to sleep.

"Well, I guess that works too," I said. "At least for now. Honey was such a good mama when she had her pups. I'm sure she'll be a good mama now too. I'm hoping we'll be able to reintroduce Griz to his own mama if Kelly can get her stabilized."

"Speaking of that, what are we going to do with the mama when she wakes up?" Landon asked.

"That's a good question," I responded. "Kelly can keep her sedated for a while, but she doesn't have a cage that will hold her for long, and she'd tear the barn apart."

"You've been wanting a wild-animal cage at the shelter. Maybe this is a good time to build one," Jake said.

"I have the perfect spot picked out, but we'll need heavy-duty steel. It'll be pricey."

"You said you had extra money after the fund-raiser," Jake reminded me. "If you can get the approval to use it, I'll make some calls and we'll put it together."

Our friends had built my new barn from the ground up in a single weekend. I had no doubt they could build a bear cage in a day or two. "I'll call Harley. As long as he's fine with it, we'll order the materials." I smiled down at Griz and Honey. Gosh, they looked cute.

Chapter 8

Tuesday, October 16

We'd never gotten around to having our first responders meeting the previous day, so it was rescheduled for Tuesday afternoon. At least yesterday had been explosion-free. Maybe the killer was done with whatever he intended to do. God, I hoped so. Honey had spent the night in the barn with the baby bear. When morning arrived, Griz was happily toddling around, checking things out, and Honey rejoined the pack for our morning walk. I'd called Kelly, who said the mama bear was doing much better. She'd lost a lot of blood, but the bullet hadn't damaged any vital organs, so Kelly anticipated a full recovery. She felt it was important to reintroduce mama and baby right away. There was no guarantee the mom would accept the cub even now, but the chance of reuniting them lessened with every day that went by. Our plan was to keep the mama partially sedated while we brought the baby for a visit and we'd see how things went. Neither of us knew much about wild animal rescue. If we were going to venture into it at the shelter, I'd need to take some classes.

I'd spoken to Harley the night before, and he'd fully endorsed our building a wild animal pen. He even offered to pay for the material so we wouldn't need to raid the shelter account. Jake made some calls and got everything we'd need ordered, as well as enlisting the help of about ten men to come out and put it together. Hopefully, we'd be able to move mama and baby to the pen in a couple of days.

"I'm going to take Griz over to the veterinary hospital around midmorning," I informed Landon as we walked the dogs that morning. "If things go well, Kelly will put mom and baby in one of her dog pens. It's not a permanent solution—an adult bear at full strength would tear a pen made of regular chain to shreds—but it should work fine until Jake can get the pen he's building at the shelter ready to move in to."

"I'll go through more old rescues," Landon said. "Unless you need my help, of course."

"No, I'm good. I have a dog crate Griz can ride over to Kelly's in. If I end up leaving Griz with her, I might head over to the bar. The meeting from yesterday has been rescheduled for noon."

"If you do go straight over, I'll meet you there." Landon looked toward the dark sky. "We've had a lot of cloud cover lately, but not a lot of snow. I keep wondering when the first big storm will hit."

"I'm putting my money on tonight or tomorrow morning. I've been thinking for days we were going to get a big dump, but all we've had are flurries so far." I paused and listened. "Did you hear that?"

"Sounds like thunder."

"Maybe, but those don't look like thunder clouds, and it's rare to get thunder and lightning when the temps are this low. Besides, the way the rumble rolled in, it almost sounded like an echo of something exploding in the distance. I could be hearing an explosion in every loud sound after everything's that happened lately. I wonder how long it will take before I stop jumping at every noise."

"Probably quite a while. The past few days have been traumatic. It's perfectly normal to jump when you hear a loud noise given the circumstances."

When we arrived at the spot where the dogs and I usually turned around, Landon looked at the ground. The snow we'd received in the past couple of days had covered the footprints, but we both knew they'd been there. "Do you know if Houston has had any luck figuring out who left the footprints you stumbled across the other day?"

"I don't think he's had time to look into it yet. He sent the casts he made to the lab, but I don't think he's heard anything back from them. Like I said, it was probably just someone cutting to the pond through my property."

I had the feeling Landon didn't believe that for a minute. I was pretty sure I didn't either.

******

Kelly had a couple of men who worked in the area help her move the mama bear to the dog kennel she used when she had overnight guests. She'd covered the floor with leaves and hay so the bears would feel as much at home as possible. Not that they wouldn't notice the chain-link walls on all four sides and across the top, but at the moment we had limited resources, so we did our best. We'd lowered the lights, so the room was as unobtrusive as possible.

As soon as the mama was settled and comfortable, we brought in Griz. Kelly had taken great care with the manner in which she'd wrapped the mama's gunshot wound, so Griz could nurse if the mama let him but he wouldn't do anything that might damage her stitches. Griz was, of course, thrilled to see his mom, but she looked a bit more cautious. I held my breath as Kelly opened the door to the kennel and slipped Griz inside. After several minutes of sniffing, mama picked up Griz and held him to her chest. When he began to nurse, Kelly and I both let out a breath.

"I wasn't sure that would work," Kelly said.

"I had my doubts too. Not only were they separated, but mom has to be nervous about being in captivity. Plus, she's probably loopy from the sedation."

"She's weak and needs to heal. I'll keep an eye on them for today. Once she gets her strength back, that cage won't hold her."

"Jake is working on getting the supplies and labor arranged to build a permanent pen as we speak. Will we be able to release them before winter sets in?"

"I'm hoping to. It would be best for them both to return to their own den. I wasn't sure she'd make it at first, but the major issue she was facing had to do with blood loss, so once I got that under control she seemed to do better right away. If we can release them before Thanksgiving, they should be fine."

"I'm going over to Neverland for a first responders' meeting. If something happens and you need me to come get the cub, just text or call."

Kelly looked back at the pair. "I will, but at this point I think they'll be fine."

I took Griz's mom accepting him back as a good omen. Maybe today would bring nothing but good news—though hoping for too much usually resulted in disappointment.

******

There were eleven first responders at the meeting: the six of us from S&R, Houston, Carl, and Donny from the police department, but just two members of the volunteer fire department. Frank and Larry made it clear they spoke for all the volunteer firefighters: None of them would be responding to any fires until the nutjob who was blowing people up was caught. I didn't blame them, but a town without a fire department was a recipe for disaster.

After Jake handled the introductions, he handed the meeting over to Houston, who opened by giving an overview of the current situation.

"I wish I could say we have a solid suspect, but all we have is a list of people of interest. The list started out with more than twenty men I researched and interviewed. There are only three left. I'm the new guy in town, so I'm depending on those of you who've lived here for a while and know the men to help me whittle things down even more."

"Who do you still have?" Larry asked.

"We have reason to believe the person behind these incidents was also here thirteen years ago. We don't know if he's been living in Rescue continuously since then or if he was here then, left, and has since returned. One of our suspects is a long-term resident, Paul Gentry."

Houston paused and let the name sit. I could tell by the looks on the faces of the men around the table that the idea of Paul as the killer was being met with a variety of responses. Finally Donny spoke. "Why Paul? Not that he isn't ornery, but out of all the people who live in this town, why Paul?"

"He made it to the list for several reasons. We believe the killer was here at the time of a rescue operation thirteen years ago; Paul has lived here much longer than that. We're looking at individuals who were involved in rescues, and when Paul was a teen, he went hiking with Trace Colton. The weather turned bad, the boys became disoriented in the snow, and Trace fell. He was hurt pretty bad. Paul tried to help him, but Trace was gone by the time the rescue team got to him. All of these things in and of themselves don't indicate guilt. Paul is still on the list because I haven't been able to track him down to verify his alibi."

"Paul hunts in the fall," Carl said.

"So I've been told," Houston said. "I don't suppose you know how I can reach him?"

Carl shook his head.

"Anyone else?" Houston asked. No one spoke up.

"Surely he isn't the only man you suspect," Larry said.

"No, there are two others, although by the end of this meeting I hope to increase that number." Houston took out a photo of a man. He held it up for all to see. "This is Walter Ryan. He's thirty-two years old. When he was nineteen he went backcountry skiing on the mountain with five other guys from his college fraternity. They weren't from this area and hadn't taken proper precautions for their trip. By the time the rescue team was able to reach them, three of the six men were dead. Of the three survivors, I managed to track down two. Neither have been in Alaska during the past week, so I've cleared them. Ryan, however, seems to be in the wind. At the time of the incident he suffered a mental breakdown. When the rescuers reached him, he insisted there'd been a seventh man named Zane, and he'd been bitten by zombies. The other two survivors insisted there'd only been six of them on the mountain, that Walter had clearly lost his mind. In addition to losing his mind, he lost a hand to frost bite."

"Quite tragic, but again, why do you think he would come back to Rescue after all this time and start killing people?" Larry asked.

"I don't know that he would do that, but I'd like to speak to him. I'm showing you his photo so you can keep an eye out for him. If you see someone you believe could be this man, call me, but don't approach him. If he *is* the killer, we don't want to tip him off."

"You said you had three suspects?" Sarge asked.

Houston nodded. "The third man was brought to my attention by one of the men I interviewed. He's a longtime resident named Vern Cribbage. He survived a wildfire thirteen years ago that claimed the lives of three adults and five children. While there were survivors, Vern stood out because he seemed to have suffered the greatest degree of long-term emotional damage."

"Are you talking about that guy who lives in the shack down by the river?" Frank asked.

Houston nodded.

"The guy's a wacko," Frank agreed. "As far as I know, he lives totally off the grid. He gets water from the river and eats what he hunts. He's never had a job, never gotten married, and, as far as I know, has never even had any friends."

"He wears a hoodie whenever he goes out, so I've never gotten a good look at him, but I heard his face is messed up," Donny said. "He was burned trying to save one of the other kids who was in that fire."

"Seems he'd be easy to track down," Dani pointed out.

"Seems like it, but I've been by his place twice and there hasn't been a sign of him. Of course, that could just mean that, like Paul Gentry, he was off hunting. I plan to stop by his place later in the evening, but for now, he's suspect number three."

I considered the list as it currently stood. Paul Gentry, Walter Ryan, and Vern Cribbage all seemed like men with backgrounds that could lead to the kind of deeply buried pain I'd experienced on the mountain the night Austin died. "How old was Vern Cribbage at the time of the fire?" I asked.

"Sixteen," Houston answered.

I supposed that was old enough for him to have been up on the mountain with Val when she died. Walter Ryan was nineteen, Paul Gentry around fifteen or sixteen. Yes, I thought, any one of the three could be the killer.

"I'd like to use the rest of this meeting to accomplish two things," Houston continued. "To come up with a protocol that can be used for any rescue or fire calls we might receive in the near future and to work together to expand my suspect list."

"I already told you, the volunteer fire department is disbanded until this lunatic is caught," Larry said. "I feel bad for anyone who has a legitimate fire, but there isn't one man on our squad who's willing to risk his life to save a building."

"What if someone is trapped inside a burning building?" Sarge asked.

Larry bowed his head. "Like I said, I'm sorry for those folks, but I have a wife and three kids. I need to think of my family first. The others feel the same way."

I saw Jake and Houston make eye contact. It seemed to me they were agreeing to let the subject go for now. Houston walked over to the whiteboard and suggested we work together to come up with at least ten additional names of men who might have the means and motivation to do what had been done in this small Alaskan town over the past few days.

Chapter 9

Jake asked the members of the search-and-rescue team to stay behind after the representatives from the police and volunteer fire departments left. Houston was going to work on clearing the names from the new list that had been generated, but if you asked me, none of the people who'd been added to the list were as strong as the three he already had.

"This is bad," Jordan said.

"The town needs a fire department," Dani agreed.

"You can't really blame the guys who volunteer their time putting out fires for not wanting to put themselves at risk," Sarge said.

"We need to find this man and find him quick," Jake asserted.

Landon sat back in his chair studying the whiteboard. "I think it might be up to us to solve this thing. I didn't sense a huge commitment from either Houston's men or the volunteer firefighters. In fact, they all seemed to want to distance themselves from the situation."

"Houston will do what needs to be done," I said. "We can count on him."

"We need to dig deeper into these old rescues," Jake said.

Jordan stood up. "You know you can count on me to help, but I need to get back to the hospital." She glanced at Jake. "I'll come back after my shift."

Jake nodded.

Dani stood as well. "As much as I hate to bail, I have a charter, and for some annoying reason, the power company seems to think it's about time I pay my already overdue bill."

"Totally understandable," Jake said. "Check in later and I'll give you an update."

I looked at Jake, Landon, and Sarge. "I guess it's up to us."

Sarge stood as well. "I have a doctor's appointment I've already put off twice. I shouldn't be long; a couple of hours at the most. I'll check in when I'm done."

And then there were three.

"So, what now?" I asked.

Landon took out his laptop from his backpack. "We have data, and much of it seems relevant. We just need to dig a little deeper. We need to sort and categorize what we find and start to develop a profile."

Seemed like a Landon thing to do, so I glanced at Jake. I couldn't help but notice he was frowning, and I wondered what was on his mind. I was about to ask him when he slid the photo Houston had brought of Walter Ryan in front of me. I lifted a brow.

"During a rescue, you usually begin by studying a photo in association with a name. Do you think that would work in this case?"

I pulled back a bit. "You want me to try to connect with the killer?"

"You've done it before. We have three names. We can get photos of the other two because they're locals, or it might be enough for you to conjure up their images. Do you think if you take some time to really focus in, you'll begin to pick up something? We only need a glimmer. A small spark of recognition to point us in a direction."

Landon looked up from the computer. "I don't know, Jake. It seems like a lot to ask. I want to find this guy as much as anyone, but I don't want to send Harmony over the edge in the process. I can't even imagine the sort of thing that must be floating around in this guy's head."

Jake took my hand. He looked directly at me. "I don't disagree with Landon, but this guy has killed two men and put four others in the hospital. He's totally disrupted everyday life in our town, and if that isn't enough, he seems to be hyper focused on you. We need to figure out who we're dealing with."

"None of these three fit the description Serena gave Houston of the man who dropped off the first photo," I said. "Maybe we're dealing with someone else entirely."

"Maybe," Jake acknowledged. "But we've discussed the fact that the man who dropped off the photo could just have been a courier."

I picked up the one suspect photo we had. "I don't think this will work. My gift is meant to save those in need of rescue."

"The man you connected with on the mountain," Jake said. "Did he seem like he needed to be rescued?"

"Physically, no. Mentally and emotionally, more than anyone I've ever connected with. That man is living with some serious pain."

"Paul Gentry watched his best friend die. Walter Ryan was so damaged by his experience, he suffered a psychic break. Vern Cribbage was burned in a fire that killed eight people in his group. Is it your opinion that any of these men could be suffering the depth of pain you felt that night on the mountain?"

I took a breath and let it out slowly. "I would assume any of the three experiences had the potential to cause the depth of pain the man I connected to felt as he waited for the rescue team to approach. I'm not sure what makes one person channel their pain into altruistic endeavors while another with a similar trauma turns into a cold-blooded killer. But yeah, on the surface it could be any of the three."

"So will you work on it?" Jake asked. "I'm not transferring any responsibility for finding this guy to you and I don't expect you to solve this on your own, but will you try to make a connection and see how it goes?"

I nodded. "I'll work on it when I get home, but I'm going to warn you right now, you shouldn't expect much."

"No pressure. I promise." Jake looked at Landon. "In the meantime, let's go through everything again. I want to reread the incident reports of all three of those rescues. I want you to pull any news articles that may have been written at the time. And pull any police reports that might in any way be relevant. We need to narrow this down as much as we can. Hopefully, Houston will catch up with all three men today."

"If Walter Ryan is in town, he must be staying somewhere," Landon said. "There aren't a lot of lodging properties open in the off-season. I'll scan the photo we have and send out some e-mail inquiries. Then I'll do a general search for news items relating to the three men."

Jake and I settled in and began going over the original handwritten incident reports line by line.

In the case of Paul Gentry, he and Trace Colton had gone hiking. An early storm blew in, and the boys became disoriented. Trace fell and was injured, which prevented him from walking out. Paul stayed with him until the rescue team arrived. Unfortunately, Trace died before they got to him. I was certain the incident must have been extremely traumatic for a teenage boy, but it didn't seem nearly as traumatic as some of the other rescues we'd been involved with over the years. What it came down to even more than the degree of trauma, though, was the ability of the person to deal with it. Paul was a bit of a loner. He had a few casual drinking buddies, but he'd never married or had a family. He worked several jobs he pieced together to make ends meet, which could demonstrate a lack of focus, but in my opinion, holding multiple jobs was just a result of living in Rescue, where good-paying year-round jobs were almost nonexistent. The fact that Paul's neighbors hadn't seen him for a few days might seem relevant, but it was hunting season, and he liked to hunt. Chances were, he was just off foraging for meat for his freezer.

I knew Paul casually. I wouldn't call us friends exactly, but he came into the bar from time to time, and while he was quiet, he certainly never gave off a psycho killer vibe. Of the three men, my guess was that he was the least likely suspect. I tried to remember the voice on the phone warning me about the fire at the lumber mill. It was garbled and didn't seem familiar, and I didn't think it was Paul I was speaking to.

The person I knew second best was Vern Cribbage. I remembered the incident he was involved in quite well, however. It had been a huge deal that affected everyone in Rescue: a church group going hiking in the canyon during a hot stretch of summer when a fire broke out and trapped them. The kids, between the ages of ten and twelve, were all locals. Suddenly, I remembered Vern was sixteen then, like me, and wondered how he fit in.

"Vern was sixteen at the time of the fire," I said aloud.

"Yeah, that sounds right," Jake said.

"The report says the church group consisted of four adults and twelve children between the ages of ten and twelve. Vern was neither an adult nor a child, so how did he fit in?"

Jake frowned. "I don't know. Let me check the list provided by the church." He dug into a file and pulled out a single sheet of paper. His frown increased as he read it. "Vern's name isn't on it."

"Are we sure the burns on his face came from that fire?" I asked.

Jake looked through the file again. "He might not have been on the original list provided by the church, but I remember seeing it somewhere."

I tried to bring Vern's face to mind, before it had been damaged by the fire. It seemed like such a long time ago, but I did have a memory of him. "Vern went to high school with me. I wouldn't say we were close, but I knew him. He was sort of a troublemaker and a screwup. It doesn't make sense that he was part of a church group, yet he definitely has scars on his face from what had to have been some pretty major burns, and he's turned into a total recluse, which fits the idea of extreme trauma."

Jake took another piece of paper from the file. "Here we go. A list of those rescued from the fire: Jim Teton, the only adult who made it out, seven kids, and Vern."

I sat back in my chair. "Weird that he wasn't on the original list provided by the church."

Jake nodded. "Very weird."

"I'm sure Vern never returned to school after the fire," I mused. "Of course, he would have been in the hospital for a good long time afterward, so he might have finished his education in a homeschool situation, if he finished at all. His parents no longer live in Rescue. Do you remember when they moved?"

Jake shook his head. "I have no idea."

"I'll see if I can find out," Landon said.

I watched as his fingers flew over the keyboard. His eyes narrowed as he concentrated on the task before him.

"The Cribbage family left Rescue shortly after the fire," Landon informed us. "According to the article I found, Vern was transferred to a burn unit at a hospital in Seattle. His parents left Rescue and went there to be with him. It appears a relative came to

Rescue to pack up their belongings. As far as I can tell, they never returned."

"So Vern must have moved back on his own at some point after that. Do we know when?" I asked.

Landon took several minutes to do a search with no results. I was pretty sure the shack Vern lived in was built on the river illegally, so there wouldn't be a record of it. I doubted he'd moved back right away. He would still have been a minor when Val died, so it was unlikely he came back on his own then. "The fire occurred in July. Val died in December. Do we know Vern's whereabouts that day?"

"I suppose he would be living wherever his parents moved after he got out of the hospital," Jake said. He turned to Landon. "Do we know where the parents ended up after Vern was released from the hospital?"

"I'll see what I can find," Landon said, and he began to type again.

I stood up. "I'm going to head over to Vern's shack. I have a feeling he might be there, and I think he might talk to me. All this research is well and good, but it seems that with the guy right here in town, it might be best to get our answers directly from the horse's mouth."

"You aren't going anywhere alone," Jake said in a fatherly tone of voice that left little room for argument.

"I'll take Yukon," I responded.

"You'll take me," Jake insisted.

I drew a deep breath. "You can be intimidating. We want this guy to be comfortable enough to tell us what he knows. I'll take Landon."

"You don't think I'm intimidating?" Landon asked, feigning insult.

I smiled. "Sure, in a sweet, nerdy sort of way. But you also have an approachable and cuddly vibe going on most of the time. I'll do the talking, but you can come along if you stay out of my way. Let's go now. My feeling is Vern isn't our guy, but he might know something."

******

As I predicted, Vern was at home when we got there. He didn't want to open the door at first, but I'd had the foresight to bring him a bag of goodies from Sarge's kitchen. The chocolate cake was his undoing. He invited Landon, Yukon, and me in, but only for a minute.

I focused on the one-room shack in an effort not to allow my eyes to wander to Vern's disfigured face. A lot of people with physical deformities and disabilities got on in regular society just fine, but Vern had chosen to live a solitary life. I had a feeling the real reason he lived this way was because of his emotional rather than his physical scars.

"I don't know if you've heard about the explosion on the mountain," I began, "but a friend of ours was killed, so we're helping Officer Houston look into things."

"I heard."

"There are some people who think you might have been the one to set off the blast," I continued, now watching his face closely.

He didn't even flinch. "I didn't."

I smiled encouragingly. "Okay, great. Can you tell me where you were on Saturday night?"

"Here."

Of course he was.

"Was anyone with you? Someone who can verify your story?"

Vern just looked down.

He obviously didn't have an alibi, and while I was certain he lived with a great deal of emotional pain, I didn't sense rage. "Do you remember me?" I asked. "From high school?"

"Sure. I remember."

"I know you didn't finish school, at least not in Rescue. Did you move after the fire?"

Vern's expression grew weary. "Why are you asking me about that?"

I shrugged. "I was just curious. I guess I wondered what became of you after the fire. I know you live here now, but there was some time between the fire and your coming back to Rescue."

Vern took several bites of his cake, seeming to ignore my presence entirely.

"Why were you up on the mountain that day, Vern? On the day of the fire, why were you there? I know you came back with the survivors, but you didn't start out with them, did you?"

Vern set down his fork. "I can't see how any of this is your business. Thank you for the food, but I have to ask you to go."

I closed my eyes and fought the urge to sigh in frustration. It was then I remembered something I'd previously forgotten. "You were up there in the gorge with a friend," I suddenly remembered. "I ran into you at the market the day before the fire. You were with another teenager I didn't know. You were buying a load of food and camping supplies. You told me your friend was from out of town and had brought some fireworks he wanted to set off. We talked about it being illegal to set them off here in Rescue, but you said you planned to take them well away from town." I looked directly at Vern. "You were going camping. Up on the mountain. You were going to go hunting and fishing and take the fireworks up to the gorge to set them off, where you figured no one would see what you were doing." I paused as I picked up on Vern's pain, which had grown intense. The worse his pain, the clearer his thoughts. "You and your friend were responsible for the fire that killed those kids and their chaperones."

Vern put his hands on top of his head and began to rock. "We didn't mean to start the fire. We didn't mean to hurt anyone. We were just screwing around. My friend had some heavy-duty stuff with him and one of the bigger rockets got away from us and started a small fire. He took off, but I stayed to try to put it out, but it was hot and windy, and it spread so fast. Too fast. There wasn't anything I could do. By the time I finally tried to follow my friend out of the gorge, it was too late. The only access was cut off."

"You must have been terrified," I said.

"I was, but then I saw those kids, and I knew if they died it would be our fault. One of the kids panicked and tried to run. He fell and hurt his leg. I tried to get him, but the fire was too hot. I don't remember a lot after that. I think I was in shock. The next thing I remember was waking up in the hospital. My parents were afraid they'd be held responsible financially and legally for what I'd done, so when they found out everyone assumed I was with the church group, they told me not to say I wasn't." A tear slid down Vern's cheek. "It was my fault, but I had to pretend it wasn't. I couldn't deal with everything, so after I got out of the hospital I took off. I'm pretty sure my parents were just as happy I did. I wandered around for several years before I came back here. I'm pretty sure they never even looked for me."

I put my hand on my heart to keep it from breaking. One really bad decision had ruined the guy's whole life. "What happened to your friend? The one who brought the fireworks?"

Vern shrugged. "Don't know. I never heard from Zane again."

Chapter 10

"Did you hear what he said?" I asked Landon as soon as we left Vern's shack.

"I did. It was a terrible story. I feel bad for him."

"Me too, but that isn't what I meant. He said he hadn't seen *Zane* since the fire. The guy from the frat rescue, Walter Ryan, said *Zane* had been bitten by zombies. That can't be a coincidence."

Landon stopped walking. "You think the Zane who started the fire is the same Zane who was bitten by zombies?"

"Zane isn't exactly a common name."

"True," Landon acknowledged. "But the fire was in July and the frat rescue was in November. You aren't saying this Zane was up on the mountain all that time?"

I narrowed my gaze as I considered. "Logic would say no. It would seem there was no way a teenager could survive all alone for five months on the mountain. More importantly, why would he stay up there? If he survived the fire, why not make his way down when he was able? But the frat guy said *Zane* had been bitten by zombies. It seems to be too much of a coincidence to be random."

"You do realize there aren't any zombies up there on the mountain, right?"

I glared at Landon. "I didn't say Zane was actually bitten by zombies. I'm just staying there's a coincidence we should check out."

Landon took my hand and began walking again. "It does warrant some additional research. I guess we should have asked Vern what Zane's last name was."

"Hudson."

Landon lifted a brow. "And you know this how?"

"He thought it. Vern, I mean. When he said he hadn't seen Zane since the fire, an image of Zane Hudson flashed through his mind."

Landon stopped walking again. "So you did it. You read his mind."

I frowned. "Yeah," I groaned. "I guess I did."

"You make it sound like that was a bad thing."

"That's because it *was* a bad thing." I looked directly at Landon. "Would you want to walk around with other people's thoughts in your head?"

"No," Landon admitted. "I guess not." He started walking again. "I'm sure you just picked up on his thoughts because you were empathizing with him, which, by the way, was amazing. You really seemed to know how he felt and you got a lot out of him. Even though he doesn't have an alibi for this week, I think we can safely take him off the list of suspects."

"Yeah. He's in pain, but he's created his own form of penance for his sins, and he lives it every day. I didn't sense he saw himself as a victim. Besides, when we connected, however briefly, I could sense a totally different energy. Vern isn't our guy."

"So I guess that leaves Paul or Walter."

"Or the zombies," I teased.

******

Landon and I took the dogs for a walk before we started back in on our research. I'd called Houston and given him my opinion that Vern wasn't our guy, and he was close to clearing his list as well. It looked as if when all was said and done, we'd end up with Paul Gentry and Walter Ryan as our only suspects unless someone came up with something new or we got back some physical evidence from either the shell casings Landon had found on the mountain or the photos that had been left for me. There were still the footprints in the snow to consider as well, but it was surprising how many men in the area wore a size twelve boot.

"I spoke to Jake while you were in the barn checking on your old mule," Landon said when the dogs had taken up their usual positions and we set off across the meadow behind my cabin.

"Did you give him an update on our visit with Vern?"

"I did. He was as surprised as I was to learn he hadn't actually been with the church group, and even more surprised to hear about your theory that Vern's friend was the Zane who was *bitten by the zombies*. I think Jake's afraid the stress has become too much for you and has made you delusional."

"I'm not delusional and I didn't say Zane was *bitten by the zombies*," I argued, feeling a bit flustered. That was when I noticed Landon's grin. I hit him on the arm with the hand that wasn't holding the rifle. "You're such a jerk."

He laughed out loud.

"Did Jake say anything else?" I asked.

"Actually, he had some good news."

I picked up a stick and tossed it for the dogs. "I could use some good news."

"Wyatt is doing much better and is being released from the hospital tomorrow."

I smiled. "That's wonderful."

"Jake's planning to pick him up and take him to his place for a few days. He wants to be sure he can get around okay on his own and doesn't overdo it too soon."

"I bet Wyatt was thrilled with that idea," I said sarcastically.

"I'm sure he was less than thrilled, but Jake isn't wrong to worry. Wyatt doesn't always know what's best for him. I could totally see him trying to do too much and reinjuring himself."

Jake and Landon had a point. Wyatt was exactly the sort to overdo. Besides, he lived in a dump with lousy heating. Jake had a much nicer place for him to heal.

"Jake also plans to reopen the bar on Thursday. He wanted me to let you know to come in for your regular shift."

"I'll be there."

"And because Wyatt will be home tomorrow, he thought it would be nice for the whole team to get together and have dinner at the bar. Austin's family chose to have him buried in Ohio, but the dinner would be the team's memorial for him."

I paused and looked up at the darkening sky. "I love that idea." I stood a moment longer. "Did you hear that?"

"Hear what?" Landon asked.

Honey and Lucky were sitting at my feet and Kodi and Juno had just joined them. I was about to call for the other three when I heard a rash of loud barking.

"We should go back to the house," I said, lifting my rifle in the air and taking a shot. When the noise had cleared, I called the dogs back.

"Is someone out there?" Landon asked.

"Not someone. Something." I pointed to some prints in the snow. "Cougar."

All the dogs responded to my call, and I suspected the gunshot had scared off the cougar, but my intuition told me to get everyone inside just in case. As soon as we arrived at the cabin, I sent Landon and the house dogs inside while I took Kodi and Juno to the barn to get them settled. While I was there, I fed everyone and cleaned out Homer's stall, then made sure everything was locked up tight before I went back to the house.

"Do you often get cougars out here?" Landon asked.

"Sometimes. Why don't you go ahead and get started with the research? I'll clean the cat boxes and feed everyone, then I'll wash up and make us something for dinner."

Landon raised a brow. "You're going to cook?"

I made a face at Landon's tone of disbelief. "I'm going to heat up soup to go with our grilled cheese sandwiches, so I guess you could consider that cooking."

Landon chuckled, then settled in at the computer. The first thing we hoped to find out was what had become of Vern's friend Zane. We had a full name, Zane Hudson. From what I remembered about that day in the market, he must have been a few years older than Vern and me. Maybe three or even five years. Landon and I had discussed it and decided he would begin with a narrow search and then widen his parameters if necessary. He began with birth dates that would make him three to five years older than me, then added births in Alaska as an additional parameter. Vern had told me his friend was from out of town, but he hadn't specified exactly what he meant by that. We needed a way to narrow down all the Zane Hudsons in the United States, so starting close to home and then widening the search seemed to make sense.

While Landon worked, I saw to my cats. Before the shelter opening, I'd taken in every stray that crossed my path. Some I was able to find homes for; others ended up sharing my admittedly tight space. Honey was the last stray I'd made a permanent part of my family, although I'd found homes for all her puppies.

After I cleaned the cat boxes and fed the cats and dogs, I called Kelly to check on the bears. The permanent bear cage was supposed to be ready to move in to as early as Thursday; I just hoped Kelly could manage with the dog pen until then. Ultimately, it would be great to have several wild animal cages at the shelter so we could be involved in both domestic and wild animal rescue.

By the time Kelly finished assuring me everything was fine with both our bear wards, Landon had pulled up his first set of results.

"I found a Zane Hudson born in nineteen eighty-five and reported as a runaway by his parents in 2001. The parents were in South America as part of a research project and Zane was attending boarding school in Seattle when he disappeared. I haven't been able to confirm that he was ever located yet. There's a photo of him in the missing persons report." Landon turned the laptop so I could see the screen. His hair was longer when I met him, and he was a few years younger, but I was sure right away.

"Yeah, that's him."

Landon typed in some additional commands. "Now that I have a birth date and a social security number, I'll do a broader search to see what he's been up to since the report was filed. If he died in the fire, I probably won't find anything. If he lived but took off, as I suspect, he would have gotten a job or a driver's license or something in the ensuing years."

"Tomato or chicken noodle?" I asked.

Landon looked up.

"What kind of soup do you want with your sandwich?"

"Either is fine."

I headed into the kitchen while Landon continued to work. I really should learn to cook at some point, but I ate at the bar every night I worked, which was usually five or six times a week. And when I was off, I normally hung out with Chloe, who owned a restaurant and so took over the cooking duties, or I went out with Houston, or Harley when he was in town. I was almost never home for dinner.

Val had never really learned to cook either. When the three of us lived together, we either ate in the bar or brought food home from there. Sarge was such a good cook, why go to all the hassle of making something different from what he prepared?

I thought about Val as I stirred milk into the tomato soup I'd picked. I missed her every minute of every day, but somehow, I'd gotten used to her not being there. Sharing the memory of her last minutes with the killer had brought back the deep sorrow, loss, and hopelessness I'd experienced the first weeks without her. The depth of emotion he seemed to feel at the moment of Val's death really bothered me. If he'd been a monster who'd kidnapped and killed her, or some random guy who'd happened upon her after she became disoriented, he might feel something when she passed into the next life, but not something as intense as the emotion I'd picked up that night on the mountain.

I'd been trying to figure out who'd be affected by her death in quite that way. Sure, the search-and-rescue team members were devastated, but I sensed a level of hopelessness and despair I couldn't quite reconcile with anyone other than Jake and me. I understood why Houston had put men like Vern Cribbage, Walter Ryan, and Paul Gentry on his suspect list, but none of them even knew her beyond as a casual acquaintance. Something wasn't adding up.

"Any luck?" I asked Landon as I turned down the heat on the soup to low and put the bread for the sandwiches on the grill.

"Not so far. It's early in my search, but the missing persons report filed by Zane's parents is the last mention of him I've come across. It's occurred to me that he might have changed his name if he managed to survive the fire and left town."

"If he did, we'll never track him down."

"It would be unlikely unless his image is in a system. I could try using facial recognition software, but I'll need to use my computer at home to do that."

I set bowls of soup on the table. "You know you don't have to stay here and babysit me. I'm perfectly safe with the dogs."

Landon shut down his computer and pushed it aside while I went back to the kitchen for the sandwiches. "I know. But I feel better that I'm here, and I know Jake's glad I'm with you too. We have a lot of work to do in relation to the investigation, so we'd be spending a significant amount of time together anyway. I don't suppose you have a beer to go with this wonderful dinner?"

I went to the refrigerator, grabbed two beers, opened them, and set them on the table. I checked to make sure Landon had everything he needed, then sat down across from him. I started to raise a spoonful of soup but set it back down before I'd completed the journey from bowl to mouth. "Have you ever lost someone you not only cared for deeply but whose absence left you unanchored and terrified?"

Landon paused. "No, I can't say I have. I've lost people for whom I've mourned— Austin, for one— but I've never lost anyone whose absence left me in despair. You're thinking of Val?"

I nodded. "She was the single most important person in my life after my parents died. Not only did I love her deeply, I was totally dependent on her. She was my security, my foundation, my everything.

When she died, I felt so lost. As if I'd been stranded at sea without a life vest and no idea how to get back to shore. I felt not only helpless but hopeless."

He reached across the table and took my hand in his. "I'm sorry. I remember how really bad it was for you and I'm sorry it's all come up again."

"The thing is," I continued, "in the brief moment when I shared the memory of Val's last breaths with the killer, I experienced a similar feeling of despair and hopelessness coming from him. I've been trying to reconcile that with the suspects we've identified and they don't make any sense."

Landon frowned. "I see what you're getting at. A random person wouldn't have experienced those emotions at Val's death. But if not those men, who?"

I slowly shook my head. "I have no idea. Other than Jake, I can't think of a single person who would have reacted the way the killer did that night."

Chapter 11

Wednesday, October 17

As was our normal Wednesday routine, Houston and I met for breakfast, then headed out for a training session with Kojak. We'd talked about skipping it this morning, given the circumstances, but the truth of the matter was, the investigation was at a bit of a standstill, and a few hours away from it might allow us to gain some perspective.

In terms of general obedience training, Kojak and Houston seemed to have mastered all the basics, including off-leash commands and hand signals. If we stopped now, Kojak and Houston would have a happy life together, but Houston wanted to explore advanced training options, and Kojak was a fast and willing learner, with as much potential as any dog I'd ever worked with.

"I think we both feel that while Kojak is an intelligent student, he doesn't have the killer instinct required for a full-service police dog," I said after we'd ordered our food.

"Right," Houston responded.

"He has a good nose, so we might be able to train him to sniff out drugs or munitions, but my gut tells me that his real calling is search and rescue."

Houston stirred sugar into his coffee. "Right again."

"The training required for that is really just an extension of what we've already been doing, but the frequency with which we'll need to work with him will increase somewhat. I suggest we meet two days a week, and I'll show you some games and training exercises you can do on your own as well. It takes commitment, but I guess you know that."

Houston nodded.

I took a sip of my coffee before I continued. "We've been playing hide and seek with him, but today we'll try upping the stakes. I anticipated we were heading in this direction, so I've enlisted Landon's help. He'll hide in a predetermined place, and when we arrive at the start of the path he'll travel, we'll give Kojak his scent. It'll be interesting to see what he can do with someone hiding so far away. He's done well with finding the objects we've hidden during playtime, so I anticipate he'll do well."

"Are we going out to your place?" Houston asked.

"No. There are too many distractions there with the dogs and all. I talked to Landon about it, and he's going to hide closer to his house. He wanted to go home to use his desktop computer this morning anyway. The key is to be supportive of Kojak's efforts and to give him the time he needs to find his target. He'll sense your tension if you become overly involved in the outcome, so it's important to do your part as his handler but to detach a bit. If he gets into trouble, we'll give him some help. We want him to be successful."

I loved working with dogs in all capacities, but I really loved training a new S&R dog. Not only was it rewarding in its own right, but the team and the town would benefit from having another dog to help out. Houston and Kojak had already proven to be a good team who trusted each other and worked well together, so I had every confidence this would work out well.

We drove to Landon's house after lunch. I'd called ahead, and he was hidden in the woods about a quarter mile away. He'd left a recently worn T-shirt to provide with his scent. I handed it to Houston and instructed him to give Kojak the scent and find Landon.

"This is Landon. Find Landon," Houston said to Kojak, presenting him with the T-shirt as I looked on. I knew where Landon was, but I hadn't told Houston. I didn't want him to inadvertently offer clues that a smart dog like Kojak was sure to pick up.

Kojak had a couple of false starts, but after the T-shirt had been presented for the third time, Kojak picked up the scent and was off. We rewarded Kojak for positive movement toward the objective, and it didn't take long at all for him to find Landon, sitting on a bench near a small lake where a lot of folks liked to fish in the summer and ice-skate in the winter.

"Good job, Kojak." I gave the dog a full body rub. "And good job, Houston." I turned to hug him.

"Hey, what about me?" Landon asked.

I hugged him as well. "You were the perfect body, except for the fact that you were sitting up reading and not laying down pretending to be injured, as we discussed."

Landon shrugged. "You took a long time and I was bored. Besides, I wanted to go over the data I found this morning."

"Something important to our case?" I asked.

"Maybe. Let's go to the house and I'll fill you in."

I looked at Houston. "Can you come too?"

Houston clipped Kojak's leash into place. "I have some time. Lead the way."

Landon lived in a small, sparsely decorated cabin that screamed bachelor pad. Most of the tables, including the dining table, were cluttered with computers, monitors, external drives, and other techy stuff. At least the sofa was clear of clutter, which was where Landon suggested Houston and I have a seat.

"What did you find?" I asked.

"First off, I've run Zane Hudson through every database I could think of. I found data that suggests he's from a wealthy family who enrolled him in a series of boarding schools, most of which he managed to get kicked out of within a couple of years."

"So he had a history of being a troublemaker," I said.

"He did. And while I've found information about his life prior to running away, I haven't been able to find a single thing on him after the report his parents filed. It makes sense that a minor on the run would stay under the radar, but I can't think of any reason for him to keep a low profile once he became an adult. My guess is that he did die in the fire after he and Vern were separated. If he had lived, it seems he would have resurfaced somewhere."

"And the whole Zane-was-bitten-by-a-zombie thing?" I asked.

Landon shrugged. "It might have been another Zane, or even a hallucination. By all accounts, Walter Ryan had a serious breakdown as a result of his experience. I spent some time trying to track him down, and after a lot of starts and stops, I found out Walter Ryan was Peter Walter Ryan, and he was committed to a mental health facility shortly after he was released from the hospital following the rescue. I'm waiting for confirmation from a source of mine, but it appears he might have committed suicide two years after."

"Which leaves us with Paul Gentry," I said. I looked at Houston. "Any luck tracking him down?"

"I'm afraid not. I've been by his place again and again, and there hasn't been a trace of him. I spoke to his neighbors again, and they all agree he hasn't been around in over a week. It's still possible he went hunting and hasn't yet returned, but this extended absence brings up some red flags for me."

I considered what I knew about Paul. Sure, he'd undergone a horrific experience, watching his friend die, but I didn't see it as something that had scared him for life. He was now the only active name on the list, but I just wasn't feeling it. All along, I'd been sure the key to solving this was to figure out how the killer was connected to Val.

"Maybe we need to take another look at the guys who haven't made it to the list and been cleared," I suggested. "We went through the rescue log and picked out a handful that took place in the six months or so before Val's death; maybe we need to look at rescues in the six months before that."

"I wonder if the failed-rescue angle is hanging us up," Houston offered. "Yes, it seems like the killer is intentionally choosing first responders as his targets, which made us think he'd been traumatized by a failed rescue, but what if his motive is something else entirely?"

"Like what?" I asked.

"Love, money, a personal vendetta. There are a lot of motives out there; the trick is to narrow in on the right one."

"But how would the search-and-rescue team and the volunteer fire department play into a scenario based on a motive like that? The people who responded were totally different. Where's the link?"

"It seems to me *you're* the link," Houston said.

Houston could be right. The killer had called me to make sure I'd have a front-row seat at the fire, and he'd sent me a photo from each murder scene.

"Okay, say that getting my attention is the motivation for everything that's going on. How can we figure out why this lunatic is fixated on me?"

"Before the landslide on the mountain, did anything unusual occur?" Houston asked. "Did you notice someone following you? Receive telephone hang-ups? Get any odd or alarming mail?"

I shook my head. "No. Nothing. The first thing to happen was the explosion. The next strange thing were the footprints in the snow, though I didn't notice them until after the explosion."

"And after that?" Houston asked.

I thought about it. "I guess the next thing was the photo delivered to the shelter. After that was the fire at the lumber mill and the phone call alerting me to it, followed by the photo of me there."

"Has anything happened since that?" Houston asked.

"Not really," I answered. "We had the rescue of the little boy, which led us to the injured mama bear and cub. I guess it was odd that someone shot the mama bear and then just left her there to die. A hunter would have taken his kill, and a random person who might have shot the bear in self-defense would most likely have reported the incident."

"And we didn't hear anything during the rescue, so the bear must have been shot at some point before we arrived at the scene," Landon said. "Now that I think about it, that almost seemed staged."

I frowned. "Yeah. It was odd that such a young child had wandered so far away from his family. I almost feel like the mama bear was shot in order to render her unconscious, or maybe the bear was tranquilized and then shot, and once the mama was no longer a danger, the child was brought to the spot where we found him with the cub. Of course, the child didn't say a word about anyone else being with him."

"It is strange the cub wasn't afraid of the child," Landon said. "His mama had just been shot; you would think he would be terrified of anyone who wandered too close to where he was most likely hiding."

"Maybe I'll follow up with the family to see if they have anything to add to what we already know," Houston suggested.

We spoke for a while longer before Houston received a call about a break-in and had to leave. I wanted to stop by the shelter to see what was happening with the new bear cage, so I arranged to meet Landon back at my cabin later that afternoon. When I arrived at the shelter I was treated to my first surprise of the day.

"You finished it," I applauded.

"Jake said to get it done as quickly as possible," one of the volunteers responded. "We asked everyone Jake had rounded up to bring a friend, so we got it done in half the time."

"That's wonderful. This is going to be perfect. I need to call Kelly. She's anxious to get the mama and baby transferred to this sturdier cage." I scanned the room filled with friends and neighbors. "Thanks, all of you. So much."

"Happy to lend a hand," one of the men said.

After I checked with Kelly to confirm the mama bear was healthy enough to transfer, I called Houston and Landon to ask if they could help with the process. Houston's truck had a large bed, so the plan was to sedate the mama and transport her in the bed of the truck while using a large dog crate for the cub. We risked the well-being of both bears every time we moved them, interrupting whatever level of comfort they'd developed, but having them in the sturdier cage was an absolute must; the mama bear was healing a lot more quickly than any of us imagined she would.

Once the transfer was complete, Kelly hung out until the anesthesia she'd given the mama wore off completely. While she didn't anticipate an adverse reaction, you could never be too careful when it came to sedation. While we were waiting for mama to wake up fully, we chatted about the Halloween party Jake had been planning to have at the bar.

"Do you know if he's still going ahead with it?" Kelly asked. "A lot has happened since he put up the flyers."

"He hasn't said anything about it lately, but I suspect he will. Wyatt is leaving the hospital today, and the team is getting together tonight to have a memorial for Austin. If I know Jake, he'll mourn for his friend and then move on."

"I guess that's all anyone can ever do," Kelly said.

"We suspect the killer might be someone who's suffered a great loss but hasn't been able to move on. You've lived here a long time. Does anyone like that come to mind?"

"A lot of people die prematurely due to accidents or poor judgment every year. Almost every one of those deaths brings with it grief that must be suffered through by those who are left behind. But to hang on to your grief to the extent you suspect?" Kelly shook her head. "No. I really can't think of anyone." Kelly bit her lower lip. "Well, except maybe for Liam Byrne. I feel so bad for that poor man. First his only son wandered off and died up there on the mountain before the team could find him. Then his wife decided it was his fault her boy was gone because Liam was supposed to be watching him during the fishing trip they'd taken. When she took their daughters and moved to Portland, I thought he might fade away completely. So much loss for one heart to take. I heard he hasn't seen those girls since they left."

The death of Liam's son had been a tragedy that had affected the entire community. And while I agreed he'd turned into a shell of a man who rarely spoke to anyone after his son's death, he hadn't been around back when Val had died, so in my mind he couldn't be the killer. But maybe someone like him. Someone who'd lost a child. The loss of a child could very well rob a person of their soul.

Chapter 12

Landon and I walked the dogs and saw to the animals before we headed to Neverland. We both had the feeling that once the team got together and began sharing memories of Austin, the memorial might very well extend late into the evening. Better to have the animals taken care of than to feel hurried to get back. As we strolled with my pack, I shared my thoughts after speaking to Kelly, as well as the idea that, while I agreed Liam Byrne seemed to be living with enough pain to make him a real suspect, it couldn't be him because he hadn't been in Rescue when Val died.

"I'm going to say something," Landon began with a tone of hesitation in his voice. "You probably won't agree with me, but I want you to really think about what I have to say. I also want you to promise not to get mad."

I scowled. "I can't promise not to get mad when I don't know what you're going to say."

"Okay, I guess that's fair. What I really mean is that I'd like you to hear me out before you decide whether you're mad."

I glanced ahead to make sure all seven of the dogs were in my line of sight. "Okay. What's on your mind?"

"A lot of what we've done in terms of identifying suspects is predicated on the memory you shared of Val's death with the killer."

"That's right."

Landon stepped over a fallen log. "I wasn't there when Austin died, but I can imagine it was very intense."

"It was."

"I believe you connected with the killer in the split second before he set off the dynamite. Your connection with him is probably the reason Jake and Wyatt are still alive."

"Continuing to agree," I said.

"And in that instant you not only shared the man's pain but a memory."

I stopped walking. "We both know all this. Get to the point."

"Is it possible, even one percent possible, that the memory you think you shared with him was just your memory of the most painful moment of your life getting tangled up with the pain this man was channeling into his act of destruction?"

I started to disagree.

"Remember," Landon added, "I'd like you to take a minute to consider this. I'm not saying your interpretation of your experience is in any way flawed, but is there even a one in a hundred chance that the killer wasn't with Val when she died?"

As promised, I took a minute to think. I was sure I'd experienced a memory—his memory—but when he asked if there was even a one percent chance my memory had become tangled with the killer's grief, I had to admit there was perhaps that much. I said as much to Landon, though I qualified my admission with the fact that a 1 percent possibility was very, very small.

I guess he must have thought our conversation was going all right, because he went on. "Thirteen years ago, on the night Val died, you were able to connect with her in her final moments."

"Yes. It was the first time I'd ever connected with anyone. Before that, I hadn't even known it was possible."

"In that moment you were able to experience what Val was feeling and thinking."

I wiped a tear from the corner of my eye. "She felt my presence. She knew I loved her. She was sad and frightened, but she was at peace."

Landon took my hand. I wasn't sure if he was offering comfort or ensuring that I wouldn't flee as the conversation deepened.

"In those last moments, while you were connected to Val, did she ever once think of another person?"

I frowned. "What are you getting at?"

"If there had been another person in the cave with her, don't you think he would have filtered through her mind?"

Okay, I guess that was a good question. Although I didn't want to relive that painful moment, I supposed it was called for. Val had gone out on a rescue. She'd somehow become separated from the other team members. She was alone in the harshest of elements, but I knew she struggled to survive. She somehow made it to the cave where her body was found, but she already was suffering from the symptoms of hypothermia. She'd fought to survive, but in the end, she was forced to let go. I hadn't connected to her until the very end. She would have been delirious by that point but at the moment of death there was clarity. I knew she loved me and I knew she loved Jake. She wanted us to take care of each other. She wanted me to know she was at peace. She wanted me to be okay. But Landon was right; at no point did the thought of anyone else enter her mind. If someone had been with her, the idea of this other presence probably would at least have brushed over her consciousness.

"Damn," I said aloud.

Landon looked at me.

"I was so sure I knew what I knew and felt what I felt, but now I'm not so sure. It does seem that if there was someone with Val, his presence would have been floating around somewhere in her consciousness."

"There's the possibility she was simply on a level of consciousness beyond the earthly plane when you connected with her, and maybe this man actually was there, but if there's even a sliver of doubt in your mind, I think we need to remove the variable of the killer being around thirteen years ago from our equation."

Finding the killer was too important to even consider digging in my heels. "That would really open up the suspect pool."

"It would. I think it makes sense that the pain this man was channeling is more likely recent pain. One of the things I've been struggling with all along is the idea that he suffered some unbearable loss thirteen years or more ago and is only now acting on it. Why now? Why not thirteen years ago?"

I bent down and gave Honey a rub on her head. Petting my four-legged buddies always managed to calm and center me when my life seemed out of control. "While I'm not saying the memory I was sure I shared wasn't as I thought, I'm willing to entertain the idea that something else was going on and the killer may not have been linked to Val or her death at all. I'll call Jake and Houston when we get back. If this guy isn't tied to the past, we have a whole lot of people to look at."

******

By the time Landon and I arrived at Neverland, the others had already assembled. After giving Wyatt the biggest hug his battered body could handle, I poured myself a glass of wine and settled at the large round table someone had set. The mood of the room was somber, which was to be expected. Jake said a few words about Austin, and then we all took turns sharing our memories of him. When we'd worked our way around the table, telling stories of our lighthearted friend, the mood had lightened considerably.

We'd just finished dinner and I was helping Sarge clear away the food when I received a text from Houston, asking me to call him. He knew we were having the memorial tonight, so I figured it must be important. I stepped into the kitchen and made the call.

"I followed up on the information Landon found regarding Walter Ryan and his admission to the mental health facility after his experience on the mountain," Houston began.

"And…?"

"While he was committed, as Landon thought, he didn't commit suicide. In fact, according to the woman I spoke to, Walter Ryan's family moved him to a long-term care facility eleven years ago. He's been there ever since."

"So I guess we can take him off our suspect list."

"Yes, but there's more. According to the woman, a man named Jason came to see him a month or so ago. Other than a few family members, Walter doesn't have many visitors, which made the visit memorable. I asked her what the man looked like and she described him as tall with dark hair and a full beard and mustache."

I took a few breaths to let everything sink in. "Okay. So Walter's visitor sounds as if he might be the man who dropped the photo of me off at the shelter. He might also be the killer. Does the woman know his last name?"

"Voorhees."

I rolled my eyes. "Jason Voorhees? Obviously a fake. Didn't anyone pick up on that?"

"The woman who checked him in isn't a horror movie fan, so she'd never heard the name before. They usually ask visitors for ID, but he said his wallet had been stolen. Walter wanted to see him, and there wasn't a reason not to let him in, so she allowed the visit. They spoke outside on the lawn. She had no idea what they talked about, but Jason left within a half hour."

I leaned my hip against the counter. "So what now?"

"I've booked a flight to Seattle tomorrow. I'm going to have a chat with Walter to see if I can pick up any new leads. I'll show him the photo we have of Zane and try to get a reaction. I have a return flight for later in the day. I'll call you when I get back to Rescue."

"I can't help feeling we've suddenly become trapped in a cheesy horror flick."

"The plot might seem cheesy, but the deaths of two men are real. And there's something else."

I closed my eyes. I didn't want to know what that might be. From the tone of Houston's voice, I wasn't expecting it to be good.

"A pair of hikers found a body in the woods this afternoon. The victim had been sitting, or possibly standing, near a stick of dynamite when it exploded."

I groaned. "Do you know who the victim was?"

"Not yet. The body is in pretty bad shape."

"Do you know when he died?"

"Not for sure, but the medical examiner thinks he's been dead since yesterday. Probably yesterday morning."

I remembered the rumbling I'd heard when Landon and I were on our walk yesterday. "Did this explosion occur anywhere near my cabin?"

"Less than half a mile away."

Damn, damn, damn. Normally, I don't like to curse, but there were times when cursing, even the silent, in-your-head kind, seemed to be required. "Okay, so we know that in addition to the killer being linked somehow to me, and possibly to Val, he was also linked in some way to Walter Ryan. The only person I can think of is…"

"Zane who was bitten by a zombie," Houston finished.

I let out a long sigh of frustration. "That actually does make sense. Sort of. If we can confirm the Zane who was bitten by a zombie is the same one who started the church fire, I think we can make the leap that he's most likely the killer."

"I had a similar thought. Zane Hudson brought fireworks to Rescue when he came to visit his buddy, Vern Cribbage. Vern told you they went up the mountain to set them off, which resulted in a fire that killed the kids and counselors. Vern was badly burned, and his friend Zane took off, never to be seen by him again. It makes sense he would have been burned too, which could have left him disfigured, which might make him look like a zombie to a traumatized Walter Ryan."

"I suppose it's possible Walter somehow became separated from his fraternity buddies because he was the only one who reported seeing Zane," I added. "When he was rescued, he told the team he saw Zane, but everyone assumed he was just delirious. He might have believed he'd seen a real zombie."

"Sounds possible," Houston agreed. "My main question with this theory is whether it was possible for Zane to survive on the mountain all that time. The fire was in July; the frat rescue was in November. And Val died in December. Even if he came down off the mountain after Val died, could he have lived there for six months?"

"It wouldn't have been easy, but Vern did say he and Zane had been camping. He also mentioned hunting and fishing. That would mean he had basic supplies to stay warm, forage for food, and cook it. The elements can be brutal, but Val was found inside a cave. I suppose it's possible Zane was living in that cave. He was young and strong and had been on his own for quite a while, so he'd probably learned how to make do with what he had. I'm not sure how he handled it if he was burned in the fire, though. It seems burns would have required treatment, but he could have had some medical supplies, and maybe he wasn't burned as badly as Vern. If you're asking if it's possible Zane survived on the mountain for six months, I'd say yes."

"Okay, so the question is, where has he been in the thirteen years since Val died, and why is he back now?"

"The real question is, how do we catch him and make him pay for what he's done to our friends, our team, and this town."

Chapter 13

Friday, October 19

The bar was busy last night, partially due, I suspect, to the fact that it had been closed for several days, but mostly to everyone's curiosity about what was going on with the team as a result of the explosion and the loss of one of our own. Jake hadn't wanted to kick anyone out, so instead of getting off at ten, I'd worked until after midnight. I'd had a text from Houston, letting me know he was back from Seattle with news. He promised to get together this morning to talk.

After my terribly long day yesterday I was exhausted, but I still had dogs to walk and chores to do, so I pulled myself out of bed. By the time I stumbled out of my bedroom, Landon had a cup of coffee and a big sugary doughnut waiting for me. "You went out for doughnuts?"

"Chloe dropped them off. She wanted to check in on you, but when I told her you were still sleeping, she said I should let you rest and she'd call you later."

I took a huge bite of the soft, sugary treat. Somehow, the luxury made the day seem almost manageable. "I appreciate the coffee, and the doughnut, but I'm wondering if you're planning to live with me forever. It's been almost a week."

"Forever, no. Until the man who killed Austin is found and captured, definitely."

I sat down at the table, lifted my coffee cup, and took a long gulp. Oh, that was good. "This is heaven, but I need to take the dogs for their morning walk. It's so late, I'm surprised they aren't whining to go out."

"I walked them already. Fed them too."

I smiled. "Really? You did all that for me?"

"For them, actually, but yeah. Homer and the rabbits have been fed as well, so enjoy your coffee."

"Did you lock the barn up good and tight? I found more cougar prints yesterday."

"I closed everything up just the way you showed me."

I felt myself begin to relax. It was nice to be able to ease into my day. I liked living alone, but every now and then I realized that having another person around to help out with chores might be nice. Of course, all the other stuff that came with having someone else underfoot twenty-four seven hardly seemed worth it.

"You left your cell on the kitchen counter," Landon said. "I noticed you had a missed call and a text from Houston. I wasn't sure if it was urgent and I didn't want to wake you, so I called him back myself. He wants to stop by when you're up and about."

I lifted my arms over my head and yawned. "Thanks. I'll call him and tell him to come by in an hour. Will you be able to join us?"

"I'll be here."

"I'll call Jake too. If Houston has news, he'll want to get an update. I'm going to jump in the shower after that. I can't wait to find out what Houston found out."

******

"First, I showed Walter the photo of Zane Hudson from the missing persons report, and he confirmed that was probably who he saw on the mountain, although that Zane's face was badly scarred, and when he ran into him, he was pretty far out of it."

"What do you mean by *ran into him*?" I asked. "Was Zane out for a stroll in the storm?"

"Walter wasn't sure. He remembers being separated from his friends. He remembers being weak and dizzy. He thinks he must have passed out. After that, he remembers being in a dark place with only a fire for light. He remembers seeing a man who looked like a zombie. He said he's tried to piece it all together but has been unable to do so. I noticed when he feels pressured, he starts to retreat into himself, so the conversation was tricky. There were several moments when he was talking to me one minute and almost completely catatonic the next. It was pretty freaky. He did seem to be able to pull himself back to reality eventually, but I didn't want to push too hard. It took me hours to get just a little bit out of him."

"So maybe Walter did pass out in the snow, and maybe Zane found him and brought him to his cave."

"That would be my guess."

"If Walter was in Zane's cave when he was rescued, why didn't the team see him too?"

"Walter wasn't in a cave when he was rescued," Landon said. "I have the debrief report right here. He was passed out in the snow and close to death when he was found."

"Who rescued him?" I asked.

"Val and Devon. The rescue party broke up into pairs once it became clear the stranded boys weren't all together. I was teamed up with Jordan and Jake was with Dani. Wyatt was with Brian Green," Landon said, referring to someone who had since left the team.

"Okay, so maybe Zane saw the rescue party approaching and put Walter back out into the snow so the team could find him," I speculated.

"It does sound as if Zane found Walter and tried to help him," Jake agreed, "and I suppose I can understand his desire to remain hidden. It sounds like he might have saved Walter's life."

Houston nodded. "Based on Walter's memory of the event, I would concur."

"So how did he get from saving Walter's life to taking a bunch of lives thirteen years later?" Landon asked.

"And what does this have to do with Val?" Jake added.

Houston tilted his head slightly. "I wish I knew. To be honest, my conversation with Walter was pretty disjointed, so I'm not even a hundred percent sure things went down the way we think. The scenario we just discussed is my best guess at this point."

We all fell into silence as we tried to work things through in our heads. I had to admit that by this point I was more than just a bit confused. Was this man with Val when she died? Or, as Landon speculated, might my memories have gotten tangled up? I needed time to think. "Did Walter say what his visitor came to talk to him about?"

"He thought the man might have been someone who lived here at the time of the rescue. He wanted to know about you," Houston said.

"Me?" I screeched.

"He hoped Walter knew you back then. He said he didn't know your name, but he knew Val had a sister and hoped Walter knew her name."

"So he did know Val," Jake said.

"It sounds like it," Houston answered. "Walter said he wanted to know if you still lived in Rescue and how he might find you. Walter told him he didn't know any of the rescuers. The man thanked him and left."

"I wonder how he even knew where to find Walter," Jake said.

"I don't know," Houston said. "Walter didn't know either."

"Did Walter have any other information about him?" I asked.

"He didn't seem to know anything, and, like I said, it didn't work to push too hard," Houston answered.

"It sounds as if we're back to zero," Jake commented.

Houston leaned forward slightly. "Not necessarily. I think we're pretty close to accepting that Zane is the killer. Walter was unable or unwilling to say definitively whether the man who came to see him was the one who helped him in the storm, but from everything we've learned, I don't think it would be too big a leap to make that assumption."

"So how do we find him?" I asked.

"I've got feelers out all over this area. I figure if he's been in Rescue for the past week, he must be staying somewhere. Someone must have seen him."

"And we have no idea where he's been for the past thirteen years?" Jake asked.

"No, not yet. I do wonder why he's here. Thirteen years seems like a long time to remain off the radar."

"Yeah, that part is bothering me as well," I said. "It sounds like he helped Walter. If he was with Val, we don't know whether he was trying to help her or not, but because he did try to help Walter, maybe he brought her to the cave to help her."

"The cave was empty except for Val's body when we found her," Jake pointed out.

I shrugged. "Maybe he tried to help her, but she died anyway. Maybe he decided to head down the mountain before he was trapped up there for the winter."

"I have no doubt anyone living on the mountain would make that decision after that huge storm," Landon agreed.

"Say you're right," Jake said. "Say he found Val in the storm and tried to help her. Say she died anyway and he realized he needed to get down off the mountain before it was too late. Where did he go? Where has he been for thirteen years? And why is he back now?"

He was asking the same questions we'd all asked. But there didn't seem to be an answer. "Anything else we know?" I asked Houston.

Houston nodded. "The body the hikers found belonged to Jeter Conrad."

"Oh no. I know Jeter," I said. "He lived just down the road from me. He liked to fish in the pond just beyond my property, so the dogs and I ran into him from time to time when we took extra-long walks beyond the property line."

"We found a fishing pole near the body," Houston added. "My theory is that Conrad came to the pond to fish and saw the killer lurking about. He might have confronted him, possibly threatened to call the police if he didn't move on, and was killed for his efforts."

Poor Jeter. I hated the idea that he might have died trying to protect me from a prowler. This man needed to be found, sooner rather than later. "Do you have the photo of Zane with you?" I asked Houston.

"It's in my truck."

"Get it. I wasn't sure I wanted to try to connect with this maniac before, but I think I'm ready to do whatever it takes to get him now."

Houston frowned but did as I asked. When he handed me the photo, I closed my eyes and tried to focus. I wasn't expecting to connect right away, but I had to start somewhere.

After several minutes I opened my eyes and looked at the others. "Sorry. I didn't pick up anything. Not that I expected to. Connecting to someone who isn't an innocent rescue is new territory for me. And I have no reason to believe he's in close proximity or is feeling any fear or pain right now." I glanced at Houston. "The last incident associated with this monster took place on Tuesday morning. Do we have any reason to believe he's still in town?"

"Not really," he said. "He could very well have done what he came to do and moved on by now. But until we know for certain, I think we need to continue to try to track him down."

"I agree." I looked at Landon. "There has to be some way to figure out where he's been for the past thirteen years. I'm not sure that will help us figure out where he is now, but the more information we have, the better our chance of figuring out what he's up to."

"I'll keep looking. We haven't found employment information, tax returns, a driver's license, or a vehicle registration, which leads me to believe he's been out of the country. I'll start trying to find something in passport records, although there is the possibility he's simply been living totally off the grid or under an assumed name."

"That's a possibility," I agreed, "but we have to keep looking. Maybe something will pop."

"I need to get back to Wyatt," Jake said. "As predicted, he doesn't understand the concept of taking it easy. I'm afraid if he doesn't let his body heal before trying to resume normal activities, he's going to reinjure himself. Jordan agrees."

I didn't envy Jake the task of trying to slow Wyatt down. He'd always been hyper, and I didn't think a few broken bones was going to change that.

"Will you be in at two?" Jake asked.

"I'll be there. I hope we can close on time tonight. I'm exhausted."

"Me too. We'll close at ten whether everyone has gone or not."

Jake left, and Landon announced he was going to his house to work for a few hours on his much more powerful desktop computer. Although he'd walked the dogs, I felt the need to walk them myself before getting ready to go in to work, so I asked Houston if he wanted to come with me. He thought Kojak would enjoy hanging out with my pack, so we gathered all the dogs together and set out along the path behind my home.

"I keep thinking we're in for a major storm, but everything seems to peter out before it gets going," Houston said. "Is it always like that?"

"No. Most of the time, when it looks like a big storm is heading this way, we get the snow that's been predicted. This has been an unusual October. We've had a little snow, but we should have had our first big storm by now."

"Personally, I'm just as happy to wait."

I turned onto a side path leading in the direction of the pond. "Me too. I'd like to get this whole thing with Zane or whoever the killer is wrapped up before the winter settles in."

I paused as we neared the woods on the far side of my property. "I wonder if we should check the cabin we discovered last spring with the secret passage. The empty property was used by a killer wanting to stay off the grid before."

Houston hesitated.

"It would fit the fact that the guy seems to be hanging around here," I added.

"Okay. Let's go. But hang back and let me take the lead. If he *is* using the cabin, we have no reason to believe he won't be there now."

Chapter 14

"The place looks empty," I said as we paused behind the tree line. We were holding all eight dogs in a sit stay behind us.

"Yeah. It looks deserted." Houston took out his revolver. "You wait here with the dogs. I'm going to check it out."

"Be careful. If the guy's been here, the cabin might be rigged to explode when the door's opened."

"I'll be careful."

I hated waiting, but I knew that was the right choice. As long as I hung back, my dogs would also, and if my dogs hung back, so would Kojak. I almost held my breath as Houston walked slowly forward. He was definitely taking his time. He walked around the exterior of the house, looking through all the windows as he went, before he even attempted to open the front door. I only let out the breath I'd been holding when he turned the knob and slipped inside. So far, so good. In the back of my mind I was expecting a big bang to accompany his entry into the small space.

After a few minutes, Houston returned to me. "Well?" I asked.

"I have good news and bad news. The good news is, the place didn't blow up when I went in. The bad news is, there are enough explosives in the secret passage to blow up half the town."

My heart sank. "So he isn't finished."

"I'd say he's just getting started. It doesn't look like he's staying here, but there's definitely evidence someone has been going back and forth between the cabin and the road."

"If he left his explosives here, maybe we can use them as bait to trap him," I suggested. "We can set up men around the perimeter, and when he comes back for his supplies, we'll have him."

Houston looked around. "That sounds like a good idea, but from what we know about this guy, I have the feeling he'll be on to us. I think the best thing to do is to confiscate everything he has stored here."

"Wait." I put out a hand. "This still feels like a trap. I know the cabin didn't blow when you went inside, but that doesn't mean it isn't set to blow if someone tampers with the explosives."

"Good point. I'll call the state police to see if they can get a bomb squad out here. In the meantime, why don't you take all the dogs back to your place? I'll stay here and keep an eye on the cabin until the state police arrive."

I hesitated. "I hate to leave you here alone."

"I'll be fine. I'm a cop, remember? It's my job to hang back and keep an eye on a potentially explosive situation. It isn't yours. Now go home. I'll come by as soon as I'm done here."

I wasn't happy about going, but I didn't argue. I wanted the dogs to be safe, and as long as they were near the cabin, it was possible they might get hurt. When I got back to the cabin, I called Jake to let him know I might be late to work. I explained what was going on and promised to keep him up-to-date with any developments that occurred.

Jake must have called Landon, because the next thing I knew, he was banging on my front door. "I thought you went home to use your computer."

"I did. I'm back."

"Jake called you."

Landon nodded. "He did, and you should have."

I stepped aside and let him in. "You know this isn't necessary. If this guy decides to blow me up, the only thing your presence is going to guarantee is that you'll be blown up along with me."

He shrugged and set his laptop on the dining table. "Perhaps, but I feel better being here, so you're stuck with me." He turned on his computer and waited while it booted up. "Is Houston still at the cabin?"

"Yeah. He was going to call the state police and wait for them to get there. I'm making some coffee. Would you like some?"

"I'd love some."

I headed into the kitchen while Landon typed in his password. After the coffee had brewed, I poured two cups and took them to the table where he was working. "Have you found anything?" I asked as I set down his cup near his right arm.

"Actually, I have. It took some digging, but I think I know where Zane has been for the past few years at least."

I sat down across from Landon. "Where?"

"Prison."

I frowned. "Prison? It seems a stint in prison would have shown up during an earlier search."

"It would have if Zane had been in a US prison, but from what I just uncovered, it looks like he spent at least part of the past thirteen years in Nicaragua."

I took a sip of my coffee. "Why was he there?"

"I don't know. I most likely would never have found him, but one of my searches led me to an article from a French newspaper about a multinational humanitarian group that somehow negotiated the release of a group of prisoners from five countries. There weren't any details of why each prisoner was incarcerated in the first place or for how long. All the article really had was a list of the names and nationalities of the prisoners who were released."

"I get that this group might have done a good thing overall, especially if the people were unjustly imprisoned, but in the case of Zane Hudson, I wish they'd just left him there."

"I had the same thought. I don't know that the knowledge that he was imprisoned until two months ago is valuable to our search for him, but I suppose if he'd been locked up for a long time, it might answer the question *why now*. Maybe this is the first chance he's had to do what he likely had a lot of time to think about."

"I guess we do have the answer to that question. And who knows? Maybe being in prison is what sent him over the edge and turned him from a guy who helped Walter to survive and may have tried to help Val as well into a monster who's killed three people that we know of."

"I suppose a prison term in a place like Nicaragua could change you, especially if you were on the edge to begin with," he said.

I glanced out the window. It had started to snow. I wondered if the state police had shown up yet. Probably not. I was tempted to text Houston to ask whether he wanted me to bring him some hot coffee, but I was sure he'd just tell me to stay put in the cabin and wait for him. I could take a thermos and skip the asking, but Landon would never let me leave. I hated being managed by others who thought they knew what was best for me, even if I knew the management came from a place of love.

"I heard we could get a couple of feet of snow tonight," Landon said.

I got up to toss some logs into the woodburning stove. I had two sources of heat in the cabin: the woodburning stove in the kitchen and the fireplace in the living space. I'd thought about having a heating system put in, but over the years, I'd managed to control the temperature of the well-insulated cabin using those two sources combined with a couple of electric space heaters for the very coldest days.

"Here's what I don't get," Landon said. "It seems as if you're somehow at the center of everything that's going on, but you barely met the guy. Why after all this time is he fixated on you?"

"Good question." I lit a match and started a fire. "Houston said Walter told him that Zane had visited him to ask about *Val's sister*. I guess he thought Walter lived in Rescue before the incident."

"*Val's sister*? That makes it sound like his interest in you isn't based on the brief meeting at the store before Vern and Zane went off on their camping trip but because of your relationship with Val."

"That's the way I took it. Houston said Zane wanted to know my name and whether I still lived here. Of course, Walter didn't know. Zane left right after he realized that, so obtaining the information seemed to have been his only reason for visiting Walter."

"Do you think Val knew Zane?" Landon asked.

"I don't see how she could have. He wasn't in town for more than a couple of days before he went up the mountain with Vern."

"Maybe Val talked about you before she died," Landon suggested. "Assuming Zane really was with her when she died, which he very well might have been."

I sat back down after both fires were going. The snow was coming down even harder. "I guess she might have. If he tried to help her, she might have shared her thoughts with him. Though I can't imagine what she could have said that would have made him want to kill people who are close to me."

Landon chewed on his lower lip. "This isn't adding up."

I got up, crossed the room, and looked out the window. No sign of Houston, but I hadn't heard any loud bangs either, so he might still be in a holding position. "Do you think I should take a thermos of coffee to Houston?"

"No."

"The snow is really coming down. He had a jacket, but he isn't from around here. I bet he isn't used to the cold coming on the way it does."

"Houston sent you back to the cabin for a reason. I think it's best to do as he says. He's the one in charge."

"I guess."

Landon offered me a smile. "Don't worry. He'll be fine."

I turned away from the window. I picked up the photo Houston had left of Zane and sat down on the sofa to study it. I closed my eyes and focused, and suddenly, seemingly from nowhere, I had a flash of insight. I felt his pain, I felt his anger, but I also felt the longing. "He craves the connection," I said.

Landon looked up from his computer. "Connection?"

"He's lived a life of isolation. He's never felt as if he belonged. He's been desperately seeking a connection since even before the fire. It isn't my connection to Val that's sent him to seek me out but his connection to me."

Landon sat back and crossed his arms over his chest. "I don't understand."

"I'm not sure I do either. I think maybe when I connected with Val while she was up there on the mountain, Zane somehow was able to feel it as well. My instinct is telling me the echo of my connection to Val served as the first real connection he'd ever experienced with anyone. Zane ran away when he was sixteen. There must have been a reason. Find out what you can about his family."

Landon turned back to the computer. "If he feels a connection with you, why is he hurting you by killing people close to you?"

I stood up and began to pace. "I'm not sure. I think somehow he's learned to equate pain with pleasure. I know that sounds weird, but I think somehow everything is tied up with his desire, his obsession, with creating a situation where he and I can connect, even if just for a moment."

I continued to pace while Landon searched for information on Zane's background. My thoughts were pretty jumbled. Despite the insight I felt I'd gained when I looked at things logically, none of this made a lot of sense.

"It looks like Zane was born to a pair of scientists," Landon said. "His mother is a physicist, his father a neurobiologist." Landon paused and looked at me. "They seem normal. From what you just told me, I was expecting to find he'd grown up in an abusive home, but it appears to have been just the opposite. He attended private schools and summer camps. He appears to have had an ideal upbringing."

"Ideal? It seems to me he was shuffled from one institution or another, in an effort, I have to assume, to get him out of his parents' hair."

Landon frowned. "I attended private schools and summer camps and I consider my childhood to have been both stimulating and productive."

I wanted to point out that stimulating and productive weren't the same as warm and caring, but I decided to hold my tongue. Landon was perfectly happy with his childhood. Who was I to suggest that perhaps he'd missed out on something wonderful? Children with differing personalities might require different types of parenting. In Zane's case, I thought he craved the connection he didn't seem to have gotten. And after being burned in the fire, he might have concluded that establishing the sort of relationship he'd always longed for was going to be even more difficult to find.

I remembered that Vern had mentioned Zane liked to blow stuff up even before the fireworks on the mountain. Maybe he'd learned to find release from his longings and frustration with a big blast of energy even before the first big bang that had killed Austin.

I sat down on the sofa and tried to connect again, but it was gone. I wasn't even sure my brief flash of insight had been an actual connection. It might have been a realization. The longer I sat on the sofa staring at the photo of Zane, the more certain I was that connecting to him was the key. It seemed to be what drove him to do what he had. Now I just needed to figure out a way to use that connection to get him to turn himself in.

I was about to say as much to Landon when the entire cabin shook a fraction of a second after the sound of a huge bang echoed from beyond the forest line.

Chapter 15

Saturday, October 20

Fortunately, no one had been hurt in the blast. The state police had arrived while Landon and I were in my cabin. Given the amount of explosives hidden away and the unpredictability of the man who had amassed them, they'd decided to send a robot in to check things out. The end result was that the only casualties suffered when the explosives went off were the cabin and the robot. The snow had helped to quell the fire that followed the explosion, so the situation was contained without too many consequences, except, of course, for the heart attack I'd thought I'd suffered when I realized the earthquake I thought we were having was actually the cabin where I'd left Houston exploding into a million pieces.

Looking back, there were several very bad moments between the blast and Houston appearing in the distance as I ran toward the last place I'd seen him. After the danger passed, I'd been forced to undergo a lengthy scolding from both Houston and Landon, who thought I should have waited for Houston to come to my cabin instead of running out into the storm without my rifle or my jacket, but I was so relieved to find he was unharmed, I didn't even mind.

Now that the cabin had gone kaboom, and it appeared as if all Zane's explosives had been destroyed, I hoped Rescue would be safe from his particular form of courtship. Of course, as my lack of luck lately should have predicted, my assumptions regarding Zane were completely wrong.

"I think this is the killer," I said to Landon when my phone rang as we prepared to take the dogs out for their morning run.

"Answer it, but put it on speakerphone."

I shook my head. "He'll know." I clicked the Answer button and tentatively said hello.

"I'm at Chloe's Café. Join me for breakfast."

I glanced at Landon. "You're at Chloe's? Is she okay?"

"For now. Meet me in fifteen minutes or that could change."

He hung up.

"I have to go," I said, grabbing a jacket. "The killer is at Chloe's Café. He said if I'm not there in fifteen minutes, he might do something to hurt Chloe."

Landon grabbed his keys. "I'll drive. You call Houston. Hopefully, by the time we get into town we'll have come up with a plan, because there's no way you're going anywhere near that café."

"He has Chloe," I argued.

"And if you join them, he'll also have you."

Landon wasn't wrong, but there was no way I was going to stand by and let a madman kill Chloe. Arguing with Landon was going to get me nowhere, so my plan was to hold my tongue until we got there and then do whatever the madman wanted in exchange for letting Chloe go free.

When we arrived at the café, Houston and his men were already there, along with Jake, Dani, Jordan, and Wyatt in a wheelchair. Not only was the lunatic holding Chloe hostage, he had an entire café full of customers out for a Saturday morning meal inside as well.

"Oh my God!" I said when I saw the thirty or so people, including children, lined up in front of the large picture windows at the front of the café. "He isn't threatening to blow the whole thing up, is he?"

"Actually," Houston said, "that's exactly what he says he'll do."

As I struggled to overcome the instinct to flee, my phone rang. I answered and put it on speaker. "Are you nuts?"

Okay, that might not have been textbook hostage negotiation, but I wasn't a hostage negotiator by trade, and in that moment, it was all I had.

The man actually chuckled.

"Please," I said after a minute. "Let everyone go. Whatever's going on between us, don't hurt any more innocent people."

"The people inside the café are nothing more than bargaining chips. Do what I say and no one gets hurt."

"Okay," I agreed. "What do you want?"

Jake and Houston were shaking their heads, indicating a huge *nooooo*, but I ignored them. There was no way all those people were going to end up dead just because my friends felt it was their duty to protect me.

"I want to talk to you. Come inside. Alone."

I paused for just a moment. "Let the hostages go first."

"How do I know you'll come in if I do?"

Jake tried to grab my arm, but I shook him off. "How do I know you'll let them go if I come in?"

"Fair enough. I'll let everyone other than your friend Chloe go. Once you're inside, she can leave too."

"There's no way we're going to agree to that," Jake said.

"Before you arrived, he said the place was rigged to blow," Houston said. "I don't like this either, but we can't let him blow the place up with all those people inside." Houston's face hardened. "Harmony knows what she's doing. She has the ability to know what's going on in his mind. She's our best hope of getting him to surrender without any more bloodshed." Houston looked directly at me. "See if he'll allow me to come in with you. Tell him I'll leave my gun behind. We'll both be totally unarmed."

I nodded.

"The policeman said he'll only allow me to come in if he comes with me," I said. "We'll both be unarmed."

"I told you I want you to come in alone." He hung up.

"I'm going with you," Houston said.

"No. I have to do this alone. If you approach the café, he might kill everyone. I'll be all right."

Houston slipped one of the police radios in my hand just before I started forward. When I was about halfway, I called out to the killer, insisting he send out the hostages. In a few minutes, the front door opened and men, women, and children began to walk out.

"We should just storm the place," I heard Carl, one of the other police officers, say over the radio.

"No," I lowered my hand and replied, "Houston said the place is rigged to blow. I'm not risking Chloe's life."

"The killer is in there as well," Carl pointed out. "He's not going to blow himself up. He's bluffing."

"No," I said again. "I don't think he is." I looked at the front of the café Chloe had worked so hard to buy. "I don't think he's planning on coming out either."

"Maybe you shouldn't go in," Dani said, through the radio. "If he isn't planning to come out, it seems like his plan might be to take you with him."

"Maybe."

Once all the customers had cleared the building, the killer called me back on my cell. He told me to lose the radio and walk forward. It was the longest walk of my life, but when I reached the door, it opened.

"Hello, Zane," I said as I entered. It was dark; he'd turned off all the lights.

"So you know who I am."

"I do. Where's Chloe?"

Zane walked across the café. He opened the broom closet, where Chloe was tied up and gagged.

"We can talk when she's outside. Not before," I said firmly.

He untied Chloe's feet so she could walk but left the gag in place and her hands tied.

"It's going to be okay," I said to Chloe, who had tears streaming down her face as she passed me and walked to the door. I felt like crying myself as she went out the door, but somehow I managed to hang on to my last thread of control. I could see her join Houston and the others outside and turned back to Zane. "Is that everyone?"

He nodded.

"If you're lying, we're done."

Zane crossed the room and sat down. "You're the mind reader. Feel free to have a look inside my mind. You'll see I'm not lying."

I thought about pointing out that I couldn't actually read minds, but his belief that I could might come in handy, so I held my tongue and sat down across from him. "So," I started. "What's so important that you went to all this trouble to have a conversation with me?"

"You're the mind reader. You tell me."

I nodded. "Okay." I had a few things I felt could be of worth up my sleeve, but I hoped by the time I reached the end of what I planned to be a very lengthy monologue, I would have connected with him and would know what he was really after. "You grew up the only child of scientists who were so completely devoted to their work they didn't have time for their child. Although you craved intimacy and human contact, neither parent was capable of providing either. You did have a nanny you bonded with, but as soon as you were old enough, your parents got rid of her and sent you off to boarding school."

"Very good. Maybe you *can* read minds."

I decided to be honest. "My friend found all of that out through his research once we began to suspect you were the killer."

"I should have known. Continue. What else did your research tell you about me?"

"Once you started boarding school you never lived at home again. You developed a fascination with blowing things up somewhere along the way, which resulted in you being kicked out of one boarding school after another, but somehow your parents always managed to find another place willing to take you. That hurt you deeply because what you really wanted was for them to bring you home to live with them, but no matter how deviant your behavior, they never did."

"Is that your entire theory? The poor, neglected kid blows things up to get the attention he craves?"

I wound my fingers together and rested them casually on the table in front of me. "I'm just getting started."

"Of course. Continue."

"When you were sixteen, you ran away. My friend wasn't able to find out what you were up to in the years between running away and arriving in Rescue. We spoke to Vern, and we know the two of you started the fire that killed the kids and counselors in the church group. Vern is scarred both physically and emotionally, and I'd be willing to bet beneath that beard, which probably isn't real, you bear extensive scars as well. And no, I don't think that's the only thing that sent you over the edge."

He nodded.

"Somehow—and I have to tell you, I'm really interested in how—you managed to survive the fire and six months up on the mountain. We know you helped Walter, who'd come up the mountain with his fraternity buddies only to be trapped by a storm. I also know you were with my sister Val when she died." I took a hard look at him. "The main reason I'm here is because I need to know about that. Why were you with her? Did you kill her? Were you trying to help her?"

"You tell me," he challenged.

"I'll need you to let me in."

"Fine with me. What do you want me to do?"

I unlocked my hands, which were still entwined with each other, and laid them palms up on the table. "Hold my hands. Clear your mind of everything else. Try to remember everything that happened that day."

He placed his hands on mine. He didn't close his eyes, but it didn't matter. Suddenly, I was there. I experienced his memory like a slow-moving motion picture. He'd seen the team on the mountain. He'd watched as Val veered away from the others for some reason. I realized I would most likely never know why. He watched as she stumbled over something and fell into a deep snowdrift. He watched from the cave above the ledge as she fell. When Val failed to get up, even though a significant amount of time had passed, he left the cave and started down the mountain to the ledge. By the time he reached her, she was unconscious. He picked her up and brought her to his cave. He tried to help her, but she had a high fever and was delirious for most of the time right up until she died. I wondered if she had been sick before she even went out on the rescue. That might explain why she'd become disoriented and separated from the others.

He stayed with Val while the team looked for her unsuccessfully. During the hours he tried to help her, she spoke to someone only she could see. During the last moments of her life, I'd connected with her, but in doing so, I'd also somehow connected with him. In Val's final moments, he experienced my love for her.

"When I connected with Val, you were there," I whispered.

He nodded.

"It was an intense moment for you. My love for Val caused you to experience a depth of connection you'd craved but had never experienced. It caused you both intense joy and intense pain."

His hands tightened on mine. It was then I knew. The reason he was here was because, over the years, he'd become obsessed with experiencing that same pain-filled love again. He craved it. He needed it. He was willing to die for it.

I opened my eyes. "You have no intention of leaving this building, do you?"

"No. But you knew that when you came in. I know you could sense my thoughts, but I could sense yours as well. We're connected, you and me. I'm not sure how and I'm not sure why, but I am sure that in the moment of your sister's death, something happened that forever bound us, one to the other. It seemed fitting that because we've been bonded in this life, we should move on to the next life together."

I leaned back just a bit. I felt like I was suffocating. I needed air. I needed space. But I also needed to finish this. "If you've been seeking a connection with me all this time, why did you hurt the others? Why not just come to me in the first place?"

He smiled. "Don't you see? Your pain is the key to my pleasure. I knew we'd only connect to each other during times of intense pain. Intense pain for both of us. I didn't initially set out to hurt you, but years behind bars with nothing but time convinced me that I needed to feel that connection one more time before we left this earthly plane."

I honestly felt as if I was going to throw up. This psycho had killed three men just so he could get his jollies in the only way he'd ever found to do so. Talk about sick.

"It doesn't have to be this way," I said.

"I think it does."

"If you die, you'll never feel anything again. Not joy, not pain, not anything."

"And that would be better than what I've endured for most of my life."

I looked him directly in the eye. "I guess I can accept that, but while you might be ready to die, I'm not."

Zane narrowed his gaze. "The ultimate release will only come with death."

I took a risk and sought a connection. I held his eyes with mine as I prodded in his brain. Suddenly, I saw something he'd managed to block from me before. "Luciana would want you to let me go."

His eyes grew big. "She would." He pulled out a detonator. "I'm going to count to five and then blow this place. Run."

I got up and ran as fast as I could. By the time I reached the door, I could hear him say five. I'd barely cleared the threshold when a huge explosion lit up the dark sky.

Chapter 16

Wednesday, October 31

"I'm sorry you were hurt, but it's nice to have someone to share the gimp section of the room with," Wyatt teased me as we both looked out at the dance floor where our friends and neighbors, all dressed in costume, were moving and swaying to the latest hits.

I looked down at the casts on my left arm and right leg. "Trust me, I'm extremely happy to be here. If the name of Zane's nanny, who I suspect was the only person he'd ever really connected with, hadn't popped into his head at the last minute, I think I would have been toast."

"He did have a difficult life," Wyatt said. "I can't help but feel for the guy. He was born into a home with absent and negligent parents, but at least he had one person who truly cared for him. But then Luciana was brutally killed in an explosion set off by rebels after his parents canceled her work visa and sent her back to Nicaragua when he was old enough to go away to boarding school."

"It's true, he did suffer trauma in his life, but so do a lot of people, and most of them manage to endure without killing a bunch of other people," I pointed out.

"I'm just glad you made it out. I think the entire experience took at least a decade off Jake's life. Landon and Houston's as well."

"Yeah." I sighed. "It would have been tough to be the one waiting to see how it all worked out. I'm just glad it's over and we can begin to heal, although I feel awful for Chloe. She worked so hard to buy the café and now it's gone."

"Yeah, that was a tough break."

I watched as Chloe hugged Landon after they finished their dance. She whispered something in his ear, turned, and looked at me, then headed in my direction.

"Your cat costume is really cute," I said.

"Thanks. It's pretty simple, but after everything that's happened, I needed simple."

I lowered my eyes. "I know I've said this a million times, but I'm so sorry about the café."

"And I've said this a million times, don't apologize. It wasn't your fault and you risked your life to save mine. I'll never forget that. Besides, everything's going to work out okay for Chloe's Café."

I raised a brow. "Work out okay? There isn't a single piece of it standing more than a foot tall. How can it be okay?"

"It's okay because I'm rebuilding. By next summer, I'll have a brand-new café with brand-new furniture, brand-new appliances, and brand-new paint and flooring. It's going to be so perfectly awesome, I can barely contain myself."

"That's great, Chloe, but how are you going to afford that? I know you had insurance, but I thought you said it wouldn't cover the entire cost to rebuild."

"It won't. But I took on a silent partner with deep pockets who's willing to let me rebuild the place however I want."

"Partner?" I asked.

"Harley Medford."

I smiled. "Really? Harley's going to be your business partner?"

"Silent partner. But yeah. He felt bad about what happened, and the town really needs a place to gather for breakfast, so he offered to help out. Isn't that great?"

I leaned forward and pulled Chloe close. I gave her a long hug. "That *is* great. And I can't wait for Chloe's Café 2.0 to open."

"Oh, I like that. I might have to change the name. Anyway, I wanted you to know so you'd stop worrying." Chloe looked at Wyatt. "Wanna dance?"

Wyatt looked down at the wheelchair he was sitting in. "I'd love to, but I'm not sure my body is quite as willing."

Chloe grabbed the handles on the back of the chair. "Don't worry. I've got this. I'll drive and you just enjoy the ride."

I couldn't help but grin as Chloe pushed Wyatt onto the dance floor. Not long after they left, Houston joined me.

"Nice party," he said.

"Jake throws the best Halloween parties. Christmas as well. If you don't have other plans, I'm sure he'd love to have you attend our traditional Christmas Eve dinner. We decorate the bar and close early. The whole team usually shows."

"It sounds wonderful and it does look like I'll be on my own for Christmas. I thought about going to my sister's, but I realized I'd rather just stay here in Alaska."

"Christmas is great here. The days are ridiculously short, so there's that to get used to, but everyone decorates the town and there's sure to be snow. It feels like a holiday movie."

"I can't wait. It'll be fun to decorate my house, not that I have any decorations, but I'm sure I can buy some."

"I'll help you. We can cut a tree for your great room, and it'd look awesome to string lights in those little trees that border the lake. I think we can create something wonderful."

Houston smiled. "I like your enthusiasm." He looked at my leg. "How's the leg today?"

"Hurts like a demon, but I'll survive."

"There were a few minutes when I wasn't sure you would."

I let out a breath. "Yeah. Me neither. It was pretty dicey there for a while, but it worked out okay. I'm sorry we couldn't save Zane. I wanted to, but he was in a lot of pain. I don't think he could live with it any longer. I hope he's at peace now."

"I heard Harley Medford is going to help Chloe rebuild her café," Houston said.

"He is. Harley's such a great guy and such a fantastic addition to the community." I looked around the room. "I thought he'd be here."

"I saw him pull up out front. He's talking to Jake. I'm sure he'll be in soon." Houston looked toward the buffet. "I haven't had the chance to eat all day. Can I bring you something?"

"No, I'm good. Try the wontons. They're to die for."

When Landon showed up at my side a minute later, I realized there must be a plot afoot to make sure I was never left alone for an extended period of time. While I appreciated everyone's effort, I didn't need to be babysat.

"Great party," Landon said.

"You know you don't have to babysit me. I'm fine. Go have fun."

He sat down next to me. "I am having fun. How's the leg?"

"It hurts and you know it because you're playing nursemaid, still staying in my cabin with me even though the danger has passed."

"You have a broken arm and a broken leg. You needed someone to take care of you, and I was already there."

"Chloe offered to come stay with me."

Landon shrugged. "I suppose that might be something to consider. I'm sure you'll be happy to get me out from underfoot."

I placed my hand on his arm. "I'm fine with having you underfoot. You know that. But you've put your life on hold for a really long while now. It's only fair to let you get back to it."

"Yeah, maybe."

I leaned back in my chair and let the lighthearted atmosphere warm my somewhat battered soul. "By the way, I spoke to Kelly a little while ago. The mama bear is doing so well, they're planning to release her and her cub back into the wild in about a week. Just in time for them to settle into their den for the winter."

"That's great. I've been pulling for the little family."

"It's nice when things work out well in the end," I agreed. "Oh look, Harley just arrived." I waved toward the entrance.

"Seems like my cue to give you some space." Landon stood up. "We can leave at any point if you start to get tired."

"Thanks. I appreciate that."

Harley sat down on the revolving chair after Landon pulled Dani onto the dance floor. I reached over and gave him a big hug. "I heard what you're doing for Chloe. You really are the most awesome guy."

Harley shrugged. "It seemed like a good investment, and I'm addicted to Chloe's cinnamon rolls. If I have to build a new building to ensure I can get them whenever I want, it seemed worth it."

I laughed. "I'm sure Chloe will make you as many as you can eat. How was Hollywood?"

"Boring, but I'm home now until after the first of the year. I'm looking forward to the holidays this year. In fact, I was thinking of having the whole town over for a party, or dinner, or something. I haven't worked out all the details."

"I'm sure everyone will be thrilled to come. And I'm looking forward to the holidays too, despite the fact that it'll be a while until I can get around on my own."

"If you need someone to carry you, I'm your guy."

"Really?"

"I even have experience carrying damsels in distress through battlefields, across gator-filled swamps, and even through snowstorms."

I thought about the films in which Harley Medford the action star had done all those things. "I guess you would be the best choice in terms of experience should I need to be carried through a minefield. I'll definitely let you know if your services are required."

"I heard Landon has been taking care of you."

I nodded. "Yeah, he's been great. Jake would help out too, but he's had his hands full with Wyatt, who, by the way, is doing a lot better. I hope there aren't any rescues for a while; half the team is on the injured reserve list."

"I'll help out if necessary."

"Talk to Jake about it. I'm sure he'd appreciate an extra body. We really need to recruit some additional trainees, but after everything that's happened, people are skittish. I guess I can't blame them."

"I'm afraid it's going to be a while before people begin to feel safe again."

Okay, now I was starting to feel depressed. Changing the subject, I asked Harley about his sister, who'd gotten married recently. Just as we exhausted that subject, Jake came over to check on me, and Harley went to talk to Chloe about a timeline for construction.

"Is there some sort of a formal schedule floating about?" I asked Jake.

"Schedule?"

"I've had a steady string of people stopping by to chat. I probably haven't been alone for two minutes total all night. I figured you'd organized everyone so I wouldn't have a chance to feel sorry for myself."

"Do you feel sorry for yourself?"

I smiled. "No. My leg is beginning to throb, but overall, I feel very lucky to be here."

Jake leaned over and kissed me on the cheek. "And I feel very lucky to have you here."

"It's been a heck of a couple of weeks. A total mental and emotional roller coaster." I glanced at Jake, who seemed to be distracted. "We never did talk about the fact that Zane was with Val when she died. How are you doing with that?"

"At first I wasn't sure how I felt about it, but now that I've had a chance to think about it, I realize I'm glad she wasn't alone. I'm sorry his being with her caused him to become obsessed with you, though. Val wouldn't have wanted that."

"Yeah, she wouldn't have." I glanced at Jordan, who was talking with Wyatt and Dani. "I do know she would want you to move on. To be happy. I'm glad things seem to be going so well between you and Jordan."

Jake glanced in her direction. "I'm glad you brought that up. We've talked about her moving in with me, but I wanted to talk to you about it first."

I smiled. "I love the idea. Maybe you can build a room over the garage for Wyatt, though, because I doubt he's going to want to move back into his tiny, dingy apartment now that he's gotten used to living in your house."

Jake laughed. "You might be right about that. He fought the idea of staying with me at first, but now he seems quite settled."

I must have made a face because Jake was all over it, asking me what was wrong.

"Just a twinge. I think I'm ready to head home. Can you let Landon know? He's my ride tonight."

"I'll get him for you. Wait right here."

I looked at my leg. "I'm not going anywhere."

After Jake walked away, I actually had a few minutes to myself. I couldn't tell if I was happy or sad. Probably a little of both. Happy for the friends who felt more like family, and sad for the loss of the friend I'd never see again. Everyone had been so great since I'd been hurt. Landon had taken on the bulk of the responsibility for taking care of me and my menagerie, but Chloe stopped by almost every day to visit with me and help him with the dog walking and animal maintenance chores, and Houston had gotten into the routine of bringing food for all of us at the end of the day. The gang who volunteered at the shelter had really pitched in, taking up the slack my absence had left, and Jake popped in at least once a day to make sure I was okay.

I thought about Zane and the lack of personal relationships in his life. Connections to others, it would seem, genuine, deeply felt caring, really was the thing that, in the end, caused our lives to make sense. Without it, we were nothing more than empty shells, existing in time and space but not really living.

Up Next From Kathi Daley Books

Sample Chapter

Friday, October 26

The dark hardwood floors shone brightly as the first patrons entered the newly remodeled bar my brothers, Aiden and Danny Hart, had sunk all their money as well as all their time into. While O'Malley's had been the local watering hole for quite some time, after years under the same ownership it had begun to feel tired and somewhat dated. When the O'Malley family came to the decision to move to Boston, Aiden and Danny had decided to buy the bar, refurbish it, and make it their own.

And what a facelift they'd given the place! The scuffed and faded wood floors had been sanded and stained in a dark walnut to match the original bar which now had to be considered an antique by anyone's standards. The old rickety tables and wobbly chairs had been replaced with new furnishings in a much lighter shade. The natural wood walls, which had previously been dark and dingy, had been sanded and stained with a rich pine finish. The most dramatic change, however, was to the old back wall, which had featured a black metal door leading out to the back deck. My sister Siobhan had suggested that the brothers replace the metal door with large glass sliders, which would bring in more natural light and a new element if placed on either side of a floor-to-ceiling brick fireplace. The doors, along with the additional accent windows that had been placed along the entire wall, brought in the feel of the outdoors, while a low-maintenance gas fireplace provided a warm, cozy feel during the colder winter months.

The place, in a word, was fabulous.

"It looks like the whole town came out for the grand opening," my best friend, Tara O'Brian, said to me. Tara and I, along with my sisters, Siobhan Finnegan and Cassidy Hart, my fiancé, Cody West, and my brother-in-law, Ryan Finnegan, had volunteered to help out during this important event.

"I knew people were excited about seeing what the guys had been up to, but even I have to admit the turnout is better than I could have hoped."

"I guess the real test will be whether the guys can retain the steady local business O'Malley always was able to depend on," Tara commented as we loaded pints of beer on a tray for delivery to the tables to which we'd been assigned.

"Danny and Aiden have been customers at the bar for years. They know all the regulars. I think they're going to do fine."

I looked around the crowded room. As I'd predicted, many of the bar's regular customers had shown up and were holding court at their usual tables. Chappy Longwood was an old and weathered fishing captain who'd worked the waters surrounding Madrona Island since before my brothers were born. He was retired from commercial fishing now, but it wasn't unheard of to find him out on the water reeling in his own dinner for the evening. Chappy was in many ways considered to be a fixture at O'Malley's.

He liked to sit at the bar and chat with whoever was tending bar on any particular day.

Edwin Brown, a retired history teacher who'd worked at the high school when I was a teenager but had since retired, liked to set up camp in the corner by the window. He was currently running for island council and used the bar as a place to meet with voters and campaign for the seat. He usually showed up early with a book. He liked to read the classics while he waited for his fellow islanders to arrive, but once he had an audience, he worked the room so effectively, you'd assume he'd been in politics his entire life.

And then there was Pops McNab. Pops had lived on the island since before my father was born. I had no idea how old he was, but I was certain he must have passed his eightieth birthday years ago. Pops liked to talk about the Madrona Island of his past, and most of the regulars who spent time at the bar enjoyed listening to his often far-fetched stories.

Yes, I decided as Tara and I picked up our trays and walked through the crowded room, the regulars had shown up in an offer of support. Both Aiden and Danny were behind the bar, filling orders and chatting with everyone who came in. Cody and Siobhan were helping Cassie in the kitchen, while Finn stood near the front door, ready to take on the role of bouncer if necessary. Tonight truly was a family affair, but after this, Danny and Aiden would have to make do with the staff they'd hired, including two new waitresses, Stacy Barnwell and Libby Baldwin. They were both running a mile a minute, so I'd pitched in to help deliver drinks. I'd just emptied my tray when someone bumped into me from behind, almost knocking me onto my backside. I turned around only to come face-to-face with the last person I wanted to see.

"Monica," I said with the sweetest smile I could muster. Monica Caldron had gone to school with Cody and Danny. She'd been, and still was, a beautiful woman who'd dated both my brother and my fiancé before leaving the island a decade ago. When I heard she was back, I was cautious. When she told me right to my face that she planned to seduce Cody away from me and would offer proof that she had, I was furious.

"Well, if it isn't the soon-to-be-dumped Caitlin Hart," Monica purred.

I was pretty sure I snarled at her.

"Where is that handsome fiancé of yours anyway?"

"In the kitchen helping out, but I'm afraid that's off limits to everyone other than staff and tonight's volunteers. Now, if you'll excuse me, I have work to do." I turned and headed back to the bar, summoning every ounce of willpower I had not to deck the witch I'd been itching to punch it out with ever since she'd shown up on the island two weeks ago.

"What's she doing here?" Tara asked as I began refilling my tray with the next load of drinks.

"She's looking for Cody."

"Ask Finn to kick her out," Tara suggested. "You know she's only here to cause trouble."

I watched as the woman made her way around the bar, distributing her own sickeningly sweet brand of sensuality to every male, whether they were with a date or not. She stopped to smile at Chappy, kissed Pops on the cheek, then sat down across from Edwin, leaning in close, as if to have a serious conversation. I had to admit she knew how to use her God-given gifts.

I looked away from the woman who seemed to be working hard to piss me off and turned my attention to Tara. "Other than bumping into me, which I'm sure was intentional, she hasn't done anything to warrant removal from the premises. This is a public grand reopening and the whole community was invited. If I insist on her being bounced, I'll be the one who looks petty."

"She's on the island to steal your fiancé," Tara reminded me. "I don't think anyone would consider you petty for defending what's yours."

"I know why she's here and you know why she's here, but no one else other than family knows she's been threatening to seduce Cody away from me. Even Cody defended her in a roundabout sort of way when I made it clear to him Monica was on the island for one reason and one reason only."

Tara frowned. "He defended her?"

"Sort of. First, he assured me that even if she *was* here to win him back, she had absolutely zero chance of success because I was the only one he'd ever loved or ever would love, but then he ruined his vow of devotion by adding that Monica had been drunk when Siobhan and I ran into her while dining at Antonio's, and he was sure she'd spoken out of turn when she made it clear she was on the island to rekindle things with him after all this time. He even hinted that perhaps I'd misunderstood what was said."

Tara picked up her tray. "Men are so clueless. They see a pretty face and a perfect body and their minds freeze up, preventing them from seeing the demon beneath the beauty." She added napkins. "I've no doubt Monica is here to do exactly what she threatened to do, but Cody loves you. I doubt he'll even notice if she comes on to him."

I hoped Tara was right, but I had my doubts. I remembered how Danny had followed Monica around like an obedient little puppy when they were dating, and he wasn't the type to follow any girl around. He was much more the love-'em-and-leave-'em sort, so the fact that she seemed to have mesmerized both Danny and Cody when she lived here before terrified me. I trusted Cody. I really did. It was Witch Monica I didn't trust.

"The group at table seven wants another round," Stacy informed me. She was a single mom with two-year-old twins who had recently moved to the island, a hard worker who seemed like a genuinely nice person. It was my opinion she would fit in to the O'Malley's family quite nicely.

"I'm on my way," I answered with a smile. "I think we're all going to be exhausted by the end of the evening, but I'm loving this turnout."

Stacy smiled back. "Yeah. I think the guys are pretty happy too." She picked up her own tray. "By the way, I saw what happened. I have your back if you need some help with the she-devil."

"Thanks. I appreciate the offer, but I can handle Monica if need be."

The next two hours were so crazy busy, I had little time to worry about, or keep track of, Monica. Finn was called away from his post by the door after an accident was reported on the highway. Of course this was Madrona Island, so a bouncer was probably unnecessary anyway.

By the time ten o'clock rolled around, the bar was so crowded it was almost impossible to walk through. I wasn't sure how Danny and Aiden were keeping up with the drink orders until I noticed Siobhan had joined them behind the bar. "Who's helping Cassie in the kitchen?" I asked my older sister.

"The brothers decided to close the kitchen and focus all their energy on the bar until closing. Aiden ordered a bunch of pizzas from the place down the street and Cassie went to pick them up. She's going to cut them into small pieces and we'll serve them as complimentary appetizers."

"That's a good idea." I looked around the room but didn't see Cody. "Did Cody go with her?"

Siobhan shook her head. "I don't think so. I'm not sure where he went. He was talking to Alex Turner, who showed up with Willow earlier, but I think they left to pick up the baby from his grandpa's."

Alex Turner and Willow Wood were friends who were co-parenting Willow's son, Barrington Wood Turner. Alex had adopted baby Barrington, who was named for his biological father, which made him legally responsible for him along with his mother, despite the fact that he and Willow weren't married or even dating. At least they weren't dating in the traditional sense of the word. They were living together and raising a child, but so far their personal relationship seemed to have remained platonic.

The grandpa referred to by Siobhan was my friend, Balthazar Pottage. Balthazar was Alex's biological father, although, due to a kidnapping when he was very young, the two men hadn't been part of each other's lives until a couple of years ago. When Alex decided to stay on Madrona Island in the huge oceanfront mansion his father had given him, Balthazar moved from his private island, located somewhat to the south, to Madrona Island to be near Alex and the baby.

"Check out table twelve." Siobhan nodded in the direction of the far left wall. "It looks like someone's about to get dumped."

I watched as a woman marched over to a man sitting in a booth next to the wall, threw something at him, and then stormed out. "She does look mad. Do you know who she is?"

"No. But I think the man who just got up to chase after her is Colin Cuthwright."

Colin had attended the same high school I did, although he was a few years older than me. I think he might have been in Siobhan's grade. "I heard he just inherited a zillion dollars."

"That's the word on the street," she confirmed.

"I'm going to deliver these drinks, then take a look around for Cody," I said, noting that at some point Monica must have left because I no longer saw her anywhere in the crowded bar.

"Okay. If you see Libby, tell her I took care of table seventeen."

I nodded, picked up my tray, and headed toward the table. I like to think I don't have a jealous nature, but from the way I'd been feeling since Monica showed up in my little corner of the world, it seemed clear to me that I not only did, I can turn into a raving banshee bent on protecting what's mine in the right situation. The mere thought of Monica was likely to send me into a rage if I didn't make a conscious effort to control my emotions and behavior.

By the time I'd delivered another round of drinks, things were beginning to clear out. Aiden and Danny planned to stay open until midnight if the bar was still hopping, but I was exhausted and hoped the party would break up earlier so I could head home and fall into what I was sure would be a dreamless sleep. Siobhan had left shortly after we spoke to pick up baby Connor from our mother's place. Connor was born to Finn and Siobhan just four months ago, but already it seemed most family events revolved around the totally adorable baby boy who looked just like his mama with the exception of his eyes, which were Finn all the way.

I'd set down my tray and was about to go outside to look for Cody when someone shoved me from behind, sending me into a table that tipped over, landing on top of me as my butt hit the floor. "What the—?" I was about to finish the sentence with a very unladylike four-letter word when I saw Monica smiling smugly at me. I'm not really sure what happened next; I guess my pent-up frustration with her finally got to me, because the next thing I knew, I was on my feet, and Monica was on her knees with her right arm pinned firmly behind her back.

"You witch," Monica screamed at the top of her lungs. "Are you insane? Let me go!"

I hesitated.

"Let her go, Cait." Danny walked up next to me.

"She started it."

"I didn't start anything, you raving lunatic. Now let me go or I'll have you arrested for assault."

Danny put his hand on mine. "It's okay. I saw what happened. I'll take care of it."

I released my grip and took a step back. Monica slapped me and called me a pathetic loser, which resulted in Danny grabbing her by the arm and dragging her away.

"Are you okay?" Aiden asked after Danny and Monica headed toward the back hallway.

I rubbed my cheek. "I'm okay. I just need some air. I'll be outside for a few minutes."

I left through the new side door onto the patio, where outdoor fire pits had been set up to provide warmth on cool evenings, I sat down on an empty bench. I wanted to cry, or yell, or even slap Monica back, but all I could manage was a few deep breaths to get myself under control. I hoped Danny would have shown Monica the door by the time I went back inside. The thin thread of patience I'd been clinging to since she'd returned to the island had definitely snapped when she'd thrown me into the table. Damn, that and the slap had hurt.

After a few minutes, Cody came out and sat down beside me. "Are you okay? I heard what happened."

"I'm okay. I just needed to get away. Where were you?"

"Out in the parking lot, talking to a couple of the guys from the softball team. I wasn't gone long. I needed some air after spending the entire evening in the kitchen." Cody put his arm around me and pulled me close. "Maybe I should take you home."

"No, I'm fine. I want to help with the cleanup, and the last thing I want to do is give Monica a reason to think she ran me off. That woman needs to go."

"I don't disagree, but I can't make her leave the island. I've told her that I'm not interested in what she's offering and I'm doing my best to avoid her, but I'm not sure what more I can do."

"People turn up missing all the time. No one knows why."

Cody raised a brow. "Really? You want me to dump her in the ocean?"

I shrugged. "I've had worse ideas."

Cody chucked. "You're right. You have had worse ideas. But in this case, I think we might want to come up with a different strategy."

I huffed out a breath in frustration. "What strategy?"

"We could get married."

Now it was my turn to raise a brow. "Really? You want us to throw together a quickie wedding so your ex will leave us alone?"

"We've been engaged for a year," Cody pointed out in what seemed to be a much more serious tone than the one he'd used when we were discussing the option of a cement-boots burial.

I paused and then answered. "I know. And I want to marry you. But I'm not going to hurry things along just to get rid of Monica. We'll get married when we're ready to and not a minute before."

Cody put his hand to my cheek and turned me to look at him. "Just so you know, I'm ready."

I let out a long breath. "I know. But we have that one pesky problem I can't seem to find an answer for. And no, I'm not referring to Monica. I'm referring to your mother."

Cody's mother was insisting that he and I get married in Florida, which was where she and several other family members had moved after leaving Madrona Island. I wanted to get married on the island where I'd lived my entire life, with my family and friends. I wanted to get married in the church I'd attended since birth and I wanted to have the reception on the peninsula where I lived, down the beach from the house Cody would someday inherit and where we would raise our family.

"I told you, we can get married wherever you want," Cody countered.

"I know, but I don't want to start my married life with my mother-in-law hating me. I need another option."

"If I can work it out so my mom is happy and we're able to get married on Madrona Island, would you be willing to set a date?"

I nodded. "In a heartbeat."

Cody leaned in and kissed me lightly on the lips. "Okay. Let me see what I can work out with her. She can be stubborn, but in the end, she wants me to be happy."

"Okay," I said. "If you can work it out, we'll set a date." I leaned forward and kissed Cody slightly harder than he'd kissed me. "In the meantime, I think it's important that we continue to practice for the honeymoon. Let's go in and start cleaning up. I have a bottle of wine and two glasses waiting for us back at the cabin."

Cody took my hand and pulled me to my feet. When we arrived inside, there were only a few partygoers still mingling around. One of Cody's friends had consumed way too much alcohol to be driving, so Cody ran him home, while Cassie, Tara, and I began cleaning up. By the time we'd cleared the empty glasses from the front and headed to the kitchen to start the cleanup in there, everyone had left with the exception of the two full-time waitresses and the family who'd stayed behind to help.

"I don't suppose anyone knows what happened to the mop?" I asked the rest of the cleaning crew.

"I think it might be in the storage room," Tara answered.

"Okay, I'll get it." I figured if we hurried with the cleanup I could leave without feeling guilty once Cody returned. It had been a long night and I was beyond tired. Still, I was happy the evening had been a success. Other than the intrusion of Monica, it otherwise had been close to perfect. It seemed everyone on the island had come out to wish the brothers well, which I hoped indicated their venture would turn out to be even more successful than they'd hoped.

I stepped into the back hallway, which provided access to the back door and emergency access outside of the building but was locked to prevent access inside. In addition, the hallway led to the business office, the men's and women's bathrooms, and a storage room. The office was usually locked when Aiden, who handled the business end of things, wasn't working. While the brothers didn't have a lot of expensive equipment, the office did house a fairly new computer plus the safe, where change for the cash drawer was kept.

I walked past the bathrooms and opened the door to the storage room. It was dark, so I turned on the overhead light. A quick scan of the room revealed the mop, leaning against the back wall. The bucket was nearby, as was a broom and dustpan. I took several steps forward and was about to step over a tarp that had been tossed over something when I realized the object that was sticking just a bit from the bottom of it was a human foot.

******

"Okay, walk me though everything that happened after I left to respond to the accident," Ryan Finnegan, the island resident deputy as well as my brother-in-law, asked after I'd called him to return to the bar.

I took a deep breath and thought about Danny before I answered. The first thing Finn had done after arriving was to separate everyone left on the premises. He was interviewing us each separately, and I knew I had to tell the truth, but no matter how I spun this, it wasn't going to look good for my youngest brother. "Monica and I got into a fight," I began. "She started it and I guess she ended it too, but I did manage to bring her to her knees at one point."

"So it was a physical altercation?"

I nodded. "She bumped into me and knocked me to the floor. Once I managed to push the table that had fallen on top of me to the side, I jumped up and pulled her arm behind her back. I learned that in my self-defense class, and it brought her to her knees. She started screaming like I was killing her or something. Danny came over and told me to let her go, which I did grudgingly. I released her and she stood up and slapped me, and Danny grabbed her arm and pulled her toward the hallway."

"And after that?"

"I don't know. I didn't see her again. I assume Danny gave her a stern talking-to, then sent her out the back door to avoid another scene."

"That's exactly what Danny said happened," Finn confirmed. "Did the two of you discuss your response?"

I glared at Finn. "Really? Do you actually think this was some sort of an elaborate cover-up to get Monica out of my hair permanently?"

Finn lowered his notepad. "I don't think Danny killed Monica. And I don't think the two of you were part of some elaborate plot. But a woman is dead and you just admitted that Danny pulled her into the hallway, which was the last you saw of her."

"I know how it looks, but you have to believe Danny is telling you the truth. If he said he showed Monica to the back door, he did."

"So how did she get back in? The back door automatically locks when it's closed, which allows one-way access out of the building but not inside. I haven't had a chance to interview everyone who was here, but I called Tripp, who offered to keep an eye on the front door after I was called away, and he didn't remember Monica coming back in through the front door after Danny hauled her away." Tripp Brimmer had been the deputy for Madrona Island prior to his retirement.

I leaned back in my chair and let out a groan. "I know how it looks," I repeated, "but the bathrooms are down that hallway. A lot of people used them during the evening. The back door opens from the inside because it's a fire exit. Even if Monica didn't come back in through the front door, anyone could have opened the back door and let her back in once Danny tossed her out. All she had to do was text someone inside to help her."

"I suppose that's true, but so far no one I've spoken to remembers seeing her after Danny hauled her away. If she came back in, why didn't she return to the party?"

"Maybe whoever let her in is the one who killed her. We both know she was a loose cannon. I'm sure she made a lot of enemies, years ago and since she's been back. I'm sure we're going to come up with a long list of people who had motive to want her out of their lives, including me, and no, I didn't do it."

"I agree she made a lot of enemies. And I agree we'll eventually come up with a long list of possible suspects who could have let her back in and then killed her. However, given the fact that Danny is the prime suspect at this point, and he's my brother-in-law, the sheriff is sending someone over from San Juan Island. Mitch Bronson will take over the investigation into Monica's death."

"Mitch? Mitch hates Danny."

"He has reason to dislike him after Danny had an affair with Mitch's ex, but he's convinced the sheriff he's over his ex and the entire incident with Danny is in the past. He convinced the sheriff he's able to be impartial, and apparently, the sheriff believed him. Given that Mitch used to live on Madrona Island, the sheriff realizes he has relationships with the individuals who'll serve as witnesses. I'm not saying I agree, but the sheriff has decided Mitch is a good person to take over. There wasn't a thing I could say to change his mind."

"He's never going to give Danny a fair shot."

Finn shrugged. "He might. It's not like he'll be able to suppress witness statements or evidence.

Hopefully, someone will remember something that will help Mitch narrow in on another suspect."

"We need to talk to everyone who was here tonight."

"Interviews would be a good place to start. I'm sure I'll be taken completely off the case and warned not to interfere, so I'll need to keep a low profile. It'll be up to you and the others to find out what really happened, but keep a low profile if you want to stay out of hot water with Mitch."

One way or another, that was exactly what I intended to do.

Books by Kathi Daley

Come for the murder, stay for the romance

Zoe Donovan Cozy Mystery:

Halloween Hijinks
The Trouble With Turkeys
Christmas Crazy
Cupid's Curse
Big Bunny Bump-off
Beach Blanket Barbie
Maui Madness
Derby Divas
Haunted Hamlet
Turkeys, Tuxes, and Tabbies
Christmas Cozy
Alaskan Alliance
Matrimony Meltdown
Soul Surrender
Heavenly Honeymoon
Hopscotch Homicide
Ghostly Graveyard
Santa Sleuth
Shamrock Shenanigans
Kitten Kaboodle
Costume Catastrophe
Candy Cane Caper
Holiday Hangover
Easter Escapade
Camp Carter
Trick or Treason
Reindeer Roundup
Hippity Hoppity Homicide

Firework Fiasco
Henderson House

Zimmerman Academy The New Normal
Ashton Falls Cozy Cookbook

Tj Jensen Paradise Lake Mysteries by Henery Press:

Pumpkins in Paradise
Snowmen in Paradise
Bikinis in Paradise
Christmas in Paradise
Puppies in Paradise
Halloween in Paradise
Treasure in Paradise
Fireworks in Paradise
Beaches in Paradise

Whales and Tails Cozy Mystery:

Romeow and Juliet
The Mad Catter
Grimm's Furry Tail
Much Ado About Felines
Legend of Tabby Hollow
Cat of Christmas Past
A Tale of Two Tabbies
The Great Catsby
Count Catula
The Cat of Christmas Present
A Winter's Tail
The Taming of the Tabby
Frankencat

The Cat of Christmas Future
Farewell to Felines
A Whisker in Time – *September 2018*
The Catsgiving Feast – *November 2018*

Writers' Retreat Mystery:
First Case
Second Look
Third Strike
Fourth Victim
Fifth Night
Sixth Cabin
Seventh Chapter

Rescue Alaska Paranormal Mystery:
Finding Justice
Finding Answers
Finding Courage
Finding Christmas – *November 2018*

A Tess and Tilly Mystery:
The Christmas Letter
The Valentine Mystery
The Mother's Day Mishap
The Halloween House
The Thanksgiving Trip – *October 2018*

Haunting by the Sea:

Homecoming by the Sea
Secrets by the Sea
Missing by the Sea – *October 2018*
Christmas by the Sea – *December 2018*

Sand and Sea Hawaiian Mystery:

Murder at Dolphin Bay
Murder at Sunrise Beach
Murder at the Witching Hour
Murder at Christmas
Murder at Turtle Cove
Murder at Water's Edge
Murder at Midnight

Seacliff High Mystery:

The Secret
The Curse
The Relic
The Conspiracy
The Grudge
The Shadow
The Haunting

Road to Christmas Romance:

Road to Christmas Past

USA Today best-selling author Kathi Daley lives in beautiful Lake Tahoe with her husband Ken. When she isn't writing, she likes spending time hiking the miles of desolate trails surrounding her home. She has authored more than seventy-five books in eight series, including Zoe Donovan Cozy Mysteries, Whales and Tails Island Mysteries, Sand and Sea Hawaiian Mysteries, Tj Jensen Paradise Lake Series, Writers' Retreat Southern Seashore Mysteries, Rescue Alaska Paranormal Mysteries, and Seacliff High Teen Mysteries. Find out more about her books at **www.kathidaley.com**

Stay up-to-date:

Newsletter, *The Daley Weekly* – **http://eepurl.com/NRPDf**

Webpage – **www.kathidaley.com**

Facebook at Kathi Daley Books – **www.facebook.com/kathidaleybooks**

Kathi Daley Books Group Page – **https://www.facebook.com/groups/5695788231468 50/**

E-mail – **kathidaley@kathidaley.com**

Twitter at Kathi Daley@kathidaley – **https://twitter.com/kathidaley**

Amazon Author Page – **https://www.amazon.com/author/kathidaley**

BookBub – **https://www.bookbub.com/authors/kathi-daley**

Made in the USA
San Bernardino, CA
26 December 2018